Ex Libris

Dick McGuire

COLONEL EFFINGHAM'S RAID

Other Books by Berry Fleming

THE CONQUEROR'S STONE

VISA TO FRANCE

THE SQUARE ROOT OF VALENTINE

SIESTA

TO THE MARKET PLACE

BERRY FLEMING

COLONEL EFFINGHAM'S RAID

DUELL, SLOAN AND PEARCE
NEW YORK

A few gentle readers may need to be reminded that the characters in any novel are eclectic; in this one they are fictitious as well, and are not meant as representations of living persons.

SOOTHSAYER

Beware the ides of March.

CAESAR

He is a dreamer; let us leave him: pass.

Julius Caesar
Act 1, Sc. 2

COLONEL EFFINGHAM'S RAID

CHAPTER I

I SHAN'T soon forget that warm April morning in 1940 when the first hint reached us that Cousin Willy had reappeared full-blown in the life of our little Southern town.

Things had begun to show some signs of looking up for us boys down at the *Leader*. It was hardly apparent yet to the naked eye, things having had a long way up to look in those days, but I had worked under Mr. Earl Hoats ("Yank," we used to call him affectionately while he was in the newsroom with the rest of us—he was a foreigner that the owners had sent us from their Zanesville (Ohio) *Herald*—but it was "Mr. Hoats" now that they had boosted him to the Managing Editor's desk across the hall),—I had worked under him for going on ten years and I detected an unusual sort of satisfied glint in the heavy lenses of his spectacles that made me wonder if perhaps, somehow, somewhere down the line things had at last begun to click.

3

On this particular April morning, bright with the baleful promise of summer, I even had a definite pointer. I was beating my way back from the Municipal Building when I happened to come upon Mr. Hoats in the shade of the Farmers Bank & Trust, finishing a conference with Bubber Paysinger,—we in Fredericksville mind a good deal of our own and other people's business in the sun and shade (according to the season) of our Broad Street. We walked back to the office together.

He asked me if anything was on the stove at the Municipal Building.

"Nothing much," I told him. "They're talking about changing the name of the square."

"What square?" he said, though more as an exclamation than a question; to all intents and purposes there is only one square in Fredericksville, the one out of which rises the hundred-foot shaft of Georgia marble adorned with the figures, generous in coat and beard, of Lee and Jackson and Cobb and Walker, and above them all, the figure of a nameless Confederate soldier,—who, fittingly enough, is equipped only with a moustache.

"Monument Square," I said.

"Changing it to what!"

"Toolen Square," I said. "What do you reckon?"

He didn't turn and stare at me, but he changed the angle of his straw hat a little, which was the same thing. "But that's a three-alarm fire for the U.D.C.'s."

"It seems the square has never been officially christened anything—"

"Hold up your story on that," he said abruptly, and of course I told him O.K.

Then in the hall of the building, as we were about to separate right and left, he stopped and pinned his spectacles on something beyond a window, in a kind of gesture, as you might lean your shoulder against the side of a door, and spoke past me in a monotone: "You boys watch your step in there for a little bit and I may can do something better for you on Saturdays." (He wasn't a Southerner but he had lived among us long enough to speak the language.) "What do you get now?"

"I don't know what you mean by 'now,'" I said. "I've got twenty-two fifty for the last seven years."

This understandably broke up the conversation; he left me unceremoniously and I went on into the newsroom.

I didn't see quite what was on his mind. I knew that in the old days, under Mr. Hoats's predecessor, what

5

I had told him would probably have been the inspiration for a leading editorial calling on the United Daughters of the Confederacy to, as it were, gird themselves for battle; I saw no evidence of any such inspiration now, but beyond that, I couldn't see.—And I frankly didn't put much thought on it because it was a good deal easier to think of maybe an even twenty-five a week.

2

But I didn't get much chance to enjoy that vision either. For, somewhat like two hostile squadrons destined one day to lock in combat but now distantly sighting each other for the first time, in the midst of my contemplation of the twenty-five, Dewey Sluster at the City Desk growled "Number three" at me and I picked up the telephone and heard a strange voice say, "Hello, Albert; this is your Cousin Will."

I couldn't remember at the moment any "Cousin Will." But it is a rash Southerner who will forswear a Cousin Will, and I greeted him cheerily enough. I thought I did recall a tough little egg down in Oglethorpe County twenty years ago when my mother and I went down there one summer to visit her people, but I couldn't remember much more about him than that he had been losing his front teeth and learning, un-dismayed, to smoke a corncob pipe at the same time.

I reckoned the voice I heard belonged to this young prodigy now grown to manhood, and when he asked me out to supper I said I'd be glad to come,—which of course I was, as any other of Cousin Jennie's boarders would have been.

The address he gave me was on the Flowing Wells Road, the first house on the left after you cross the city boundary. "My name's on the mailbox," he said.

I took a Mechanics Hill bus out to the end of the line, got off and walked along a sandy road through a stand of second-growth pines with an occasional glimpse off over Horse Creek Valley at a bank of low hills about the color of a pair of sun-faded overalls. I supposed Cousin Willy had got married, sold the old Effingham place and moved to the city to make his for-tune; there were a few things that didn't add up about this idea of him, but that was pretty much the state of my mind when I walked round a slight bend and saw the new mailbox.

I felt I hardly needed to look at the name, so certain was I that this was the house, but as I entered the gate I did glance casually at the freshly-painted letters. They halted me right there like a sentry's challenge and I stood off spelling them out, certain now that something was wrong but not knowing just where it began: "W. SEABORN EFFINGHAM," the first line read, which was all right, but underneath it were the words, "Colonel U. S. Army, retired."

Then, far back out of the dusk of childhood there began to emerge a vague Great-uncle Seaby on my mother's side who had a son about my mother's age they all referred to as Willy,—when they referred to him at all, which was seldom because he had graduated at West Point and long since disappeared from our lives, though I remember he did send us boys a Christmas present once that arrived about the first of December and turned out to be nothing less than a machete out of the jungles of Panama, from the shock of which I am not at all sure my mother ever recovered—

"Is this Albert Marbury?" a big voice said from the edge of the porch.

I lifted my eyes to the sunburned face of a somehow formidable-looking figure, spare and erect and, seeing him thus above me on the steps, of an apparently prodigious height; a pale cravat was twirled loosely under the liberal collar of a good linen shirt, out of which rose a really distinguished Adam's apple.

8

Matching it for prominence, was a high and rather delicately-boned nose, beneath which a pair of aggressive yet disciplined gray moustaches turned briefly to either flank. In the same key, a pair of wiry and mobile eyebrows seemed almost to impair the vision of two brown eyes that could have belonged only to an Effingham. They were my mother's eyes and though it was curious to see them there under the pink expanse of a cranium as bald as the top of his mailbox, it was heartwarming too, in a way; what, in my mother's eyes, had been a personal kindliness, seemed to have become in his something that might be a sort of stern solicitude for the troops in his command, but in both cases it was an outward look unobstructed by much consideration of self. His bony shoulders were neatly clad in a nice-fitting jacket of some light-colored cotton stuff which, as it later turned out, he had brought home with him from Manila.

He grasped my hand in his lanky brown fingers. "Come in, my boy; it's good to see kin people again."

I had never felt that way about kin people, but I reckoned you picked up stranger ideas than that in a lifetime spent in the army and I didn't argue the point; I hadn't been as starved of them as he had.

9

"This is a nice place you found," I said.

"Comfortable quarters," Cousin Willy said modestly.

He showed me through the rooms of what we call a "sand-hills cottage," a one-storey building with a wide hall connecting the front and back porches, and two or three rooms on each side, with a kitchen wing and perhaps a corresponding wing for an office or an extra bedroom. It was an office in this case, clean and bare, with a portable typewriter on a simple desk between the window and the fireplace. I said something about maybe he was going to write his memoirs now.

"My critique of the action?" he smiled a little. "I don't know; I've been here only a week. In fact I hardly know whether to consider this garrison or bivouac area."

"But you are retired," I mentioned; "you won't be moving—"

"I am retired, yes," he said. "But any one of us, you know, may receive his transfer orders in any mail.— Oh, orderly!" then turning to me, "What may I offer you to drink?"

We settled on something; I forget what it was, because when the "orderly" appeared I recognized him, in spite of the stiff white coat, a little too long for him, and the newly-creased sleeves that he obviously sort of hated to break, as Ninety-eight, a lean colored boy I used to go fishing with on Uncle Jerry's farm up in Twiggs County. (He was named after his father, who claimed that was the temperature that stirred him to his greatest efficiency,—which wasn't saying much.)

"Well, Ninety-eight!" I said to him standing there in the doorway with his heels together and his shoulders thrown back so far they pulled his coat into a great wrinkle across the top of his chest. But he just grinned tolerantly at me, the uninitiated civilian, looking straight to the front.

Cousin Willy told him to bring our drinks out to the gun emplacement.

"I beg your pardon!" I said.

"This is a very extraordinary position," he interrupted me, leading me out through the back door and into a yard that began to drop off quite rapidly into the valley. He paused on a freshly-made path through the rank Bermuda grass and lifted his open hand in a gesture at the crest of the hill; I didn't know whether to expect a Revolutionary cannon or a machine-gun nest. The only thing observable to the eye were some grass-covered mounds about ten feet high on the lower side of the hill and circling round with their tops almost level until they disappeared. "Confederate breastworks," said Cousin Willy.

We climbed up on top where two or three sacrilegious cedar trees were ignorantly growing and sat down on a pair of camp stools with folding backs. "A very canny strongpoint," he said with a smile of pride for the profession. "You see that road over there?" He handed me a pair of Zeiss glasses.

In a far break of the trees on the ridge you could see the pink road over which one of Sherman's columns had been expected to advance on Fredericksville, but had not,—to the, at heart, considerable chagrin of the citizens, who believed that their town was of just as great military importance as Atlanta and who, I suspect, have never, since the invaders passed some forty miles to the west, felt quite the same toward the capital, having toward it some of that semi-dormant malice that a spinster is likely to have toward a wayward sister who has, so to speak, been through the mill.

I gave the road a polite glance; it was as deserted as it had been in '64. But when I handed the glasses back to Cousin Willy he steadied them against one of the cedars and gave the road a thorough going-over.

When Ninety-eight brought our drinks, he passed round behind the tree, not to interrupt the colonel's field of vision. "There could be a Cossack post in those woods to the right," he said; then possibly hearing my thirsty rattle of the ice, he put the binoculars away.

"Well," I said, "there's hardly much danger of that now."

He looked at me in silence for a moment, then he said portentously, "Any populated center, Albert, is always in danger. Call in your sentries and the enemy appears."

This was getting pretty technical for me and I turned the conversation to his retirement.

"Yes," he said cheerfully, "Uncle Sam has turned the old horse out to graze,—or I suppose nowadays one ought to say 'put the jacks under the old armored car.'"

"Oh, no," I said deprecatingly, not wanting him to be dejected that his active service was over.

"In a way, I've been looking forward to it."

"You have a lot of old friends here, Cousin Willy," I said.

"Yes, there's Clyde Manadue and Sterling and Jesse Bibb and—"

"Enough for a good Saturday afternoon poker game," I suggested.

"I look upon retirement, Albert, as merely being assigned to a new post,—and there are few more salutary prescriptions for a man's health than the one contained in his transfer orders: a new command means a new point of view, new problems, new solutions—"

I felt, in truth, a little sorry for him. I supposed he, naturally enough, wished to put the best face possible on it for his own peace of mind, but I could not see how being assigned to the Fredericksville station offered, to say the most, much opportunity for advancement. This was a quiet sector; I had lived there all my life and was accustomed to it and even I was fondly hoping to get time some day to write a novel that would call me away. But to somebody like Cousin Willy, who had touched upon most of the inhabited world in his duties, or at any rate most of it that was civilized enough to require the presence of the militia, a tour of duty in a theater as inactive as Fredericksville would have seemed to me a considerable letdown. I felt that the story of Fredericksville was epitomized in those earthworks the Home Guard had thrown up there: the expected action seemed always to pass us by, some forty miles to the north, south, east, or west.

He questioned me about the city, as if I had been a scout with blackened face just in from reconnaissance. I surprised myself at how little I was really competent to tell him; I knew the specific Fredericksville that crossed a reporter's path, but I couldn't help him out much with the Fredericksville that was one of hundreds of American cities.

"There are about sixty thousand people in Fredericksville," I said in the voice of the guidebook; "twenty or twenty-five thousand colored. Most of the white population are native Americans of Anglo Saxon origin and we live under the democratic form of government," I smiled, hoping, frankly, to disguise the nakedness of my ignorance by the confusion of humor, a little trick as natural to us Southerners as the clouding of the water to a competent octopus.

"How many Citizens voted in the last election?" said Cousin Willy persistently.

"Oh, four or five thousand," I guessed.

"Do you mean fifty-five thousand took no part in the action!"

"Well," I said, "I shouldn't put it exactly that way—"

"Why was there such a shattering percent unfit for service!"

I couldn't answer that and I was glad Ninety-eight rescued me with the announcement of supper; discussing our local democratic form of government is a very ticklish proposition at best. We get round the difficulty by creating a sort of halo for the adjective "non-political," which puts politics in about the same category as many other elemental functions not usually considered polite conversation for mixed company.

"Perhaps Fredericksville has been neglecting its history," he said as we sat down at table, without much apparent connection to what we had been talking about. "History is an ennobling study,—ennobling, as a man usually seems ennobled in death. History is humanity's death mask and on it even our errors assume some dignity. In times when you are hard pressed, to remember that your grandfather fought through, strengthens your arm; I don't see why it wouldn't be the same with a town.—That's rice Filipino style, Albert; help yourself. It looks very good, orderly."

. . . . Altogether, I enjoyed the evening. I didn't know just what to make of Cousin Willy, but I didn't try to make anything much beyond the general belief that he had been instinctively right in choosing to return to the South to pass the rest of his life. It has long been my conviction that, whereas most places upon this earth are forced back for their distinguishing characteristic upon some inanimate geological or architectural

16

peculiarity, such as the springs at White Sulphur or the bay at San Francisco or the skyline at New York, the South on the other hand, being predominantly coastal plain and sand hill and red clay, and without many breath-taking dispositions of terrain or masonry, offers more simply breath-taking dispositions of character, and abounds, from sea island to Smokies, in all manner of startling configurations of human whims and prejudices,—and I felt that, on the whole, Cousin Willy was very likely going to be able to hold up his end.

As I was leaving he mentioned to me his need of a sort of quartermaster-mess officer, and upon my suggestion, he decided there and then to employ Cousin Tom's widow, a gentle lady with an almost unfathomable capacity for listening when the voice was male, and enough younger than himself to make the chances of his having to bury her inconsiderable.

I caught the last bus into town and rode to my corner, my mind all the way pleasantly occupied with the picture of Cousin Willy more or less hurling himself into the ghostly breach between his native town and the wraith of General Sherman, entrenching himself, cheerfully pitching what he probably considered to be his last tent.

One of his first acts of course, as you would expect, was an inspection of the post. For the first few days he hired what we imitatively call a "taxicab;" it is merely an unusually well-travelled sedan with a bright legend as to ownership on each door and a circular sign on the back advertising one of the cola drinks so dear to our digestive systems. The latter part of the tour he made in a neat black Ford of his own, driven by Ninety-eight in a chauffeur's cap appropriate to the occasion; Cousin Willy sat critically in one corner of the back seat, I, for some of the time, in the other. Now and then he would raise his hand with a "Hold on, there," and we would pull up and descend.

I gathered that he found Fredericksville not very different from the town he had left a quarter century before, allowing for reasonable alterations both in it and in the eyes with which he saw it. It still spread out in gradually increasing thinness from the cross on the river bank marking the site of old Fort Frederick, built there by Oglethorpe in 1735 (and named, in a no-doubt unappreciated gesture, for the Prince of Wales) for the purpose of providing the Anglo Saxon traders and their families with some refuge when the

Uchee Indians occasionally reached the possibly quite-tenable conclusion that they had been out-traded, still spread out up and down the river and across the low plain to the bordering sand hills. The old parade had now become the main business street and led off to east and west in a wide vista, wider than the Mall, the colonel declared, and than the Champs Elysees, interrupted in the heart of the modern trading area by the monument I have referred to, commemorating the Confederate States of America.

He pulled Ninety-eight up beside it and sat there considering it in silence until Officer Bop Ginby of the Traffic Squad whistled and Ninety-eight jumped like the lead mule on a cotton dray with a whip cracked over his ears. I expected Cousin Willy to wither Officer Ginby in a flame-throwing stare, but as we passed he gave him a sort of commending half salute as a general might to a sentry who had properly challenged him.

"I thought there were trees along this street," he said.

I told him there used to be.

"There are trees along the Champs Elysees, trees on Unter den Linden, on the Mall; there ought to be trees on Broad Street."

My heart misgave me for a second. Ever since I had

been on the *Leader*, every two years or at most three, somebody tried to start a campaign to make the city appropriate money to plant trees on Broad Street; the government didn't even bother to smile any more. The suggestion was not even a bad joke; it just wasn't anything. The idea that a kinsman of mine might stir it all up again (I didn't know him very well, you see) made me a little faint.—I reminded him hastily that he had said he wanted to see the site of the old fort.

"Yes, indeed," he said, and I directed Ninety-eight how to get there.

The colonel slung his binoculars round his neck and we left the car. He stood for a few minutes in front of the cross, studying the old cannon which some people claim Oglethorpe brought with him from England; he didn't say anything and after a while I saw Ninety-eight picking himself a capful of dewberries off a bush not far away and I joined him.

When I looked up again, the colonel was standing out on the river bank with his glasses levelled down the stream. I walked out beside him and he handed them to me, pointing with his long finger at the far side of the bend; I stared through them at the empty coils of the red river, trying to find what had caught his eye.

"There," he said in a minute, "almost four hundred years ago to the day, come the long canoes of the expedition of one Fernando de Soto, paddling up along the overhanging trees to escape the current, paddling up the black water into the chirping wilderness."

"It's red," I observed.

"It was black then," he said, as if merely checking his memory; "as black as a deep spring. Standing in the bow of the leading canoe, leaning motionless on his long carbine, the New World sun glinting on the good Spanish brass of his helmet and his cuirass, is the young De Soto, scarcely forty-four, his black beard clean-combed, for he was a gentleman, his black eyes sweeping the river,—for he was a seeker."

"I can't see him from where I stand," I said.

"Kneeling beside him is a naked Indian, supple as new rubber, pointing to a clearing in the trees and a landing place (right over there), where some smoke is rising from the central hut of a settlement made of upright poles with the roofs covered with cane from the swamp.—He was looking for something, gold perhaps, adventure, fame, the prestige at home of having well served his country."

I was glad to see him putting the glasses back into their case, for I was getting a little uncomfortable. But he went on talking, though not so much to me and Ninety-eight as to the broad valley, which he scrutinized upstream and down. "Ponce de Leon, trudging through The Land of Easter, looking for a water to restore his youth. Balboa, Pineda,—Coronado searching the plains for the Seven Cities of Cibola. Everything they had dreamed of in Europe they searched for here in America; it was not so much the Indies that they thought they had found, as the land of answered hopes."

"Amen," said Ninety-eight from where he was sitting on his heels with the dewberries, his ear sensing a spiritual note.

I had an afternoon paper to get out and it is perhaps not surprising that on the whole Ninety-eight, who hadn't, was taking to all this more heartily than I was. He even offered at this point some Twiggs County folklore of his own: "Georgia, Colonel," he said, passing Cousin Willy the dewberries, "is just naturally a healthier state than Carolina. The sun rises over Carolina and it draws all these old malaria fevers and germs over there away from Georgia."

"It doesn't pull them all back over Georgia when it sets?" said the colonel in a good-natured parenthesis, taking one of the dewberries as he might sample the regimental mess.

"No, sir. The old germs come out of the swamps at night and the rising sun catches them.—I drove old Mr. Jerry up to Richmond, Virginia, and back once. We stopped and talked to everybody along the road. I remember when we got back to the Savannah River he said to me, 'Ninety-eight, you know we haven't seen a real healthy-looking man since we left Georgia—' "

"Colonel," I said, trying to edge us all over in the direction of the car, "maybe you'd like to run down and glance at the old courthouse and the old military academy—"

"That was later," said Cousin Willy. "That belongs to the period of holding the position. We are now engaged in the sweat and toil of establishing a bridgehead."

These were pretty disturbing words; I had expected to make the usual rounds of the "historic spots" and get on back to my typewriter. I hadn't come equipped to do any serious colonizing.

"Two hundred years later," Cousin Willy went on, "the same time-distance from De Soto as from you, Albert, a young general of the British Army (he was thirty-nine years old) sat in his simple tent under four pine trees on the bluffs at Savannah and checked through his roster, picking the platoon he was going to send to build and hold the defensive position at Fort Frederick.

"General Oglethorpe, of course, could not come himself. This would be an interior strongpoint for the protection merely of commerce; the principal threat to Georgia, he well knew, was not the Indians but the Romanists and he returned to his outpost on the sea where he could keep an eye on Saint Augustine. But he sent a platoon of picked troops up the river with orders to build Fort Frederick and hold it until further notice. They landed right down there by that sycamore tree."

Ninety-eight moved a little so he could see better.

"And they hauled eight eighteen-pounders up this bank here with block and tackle."

"Them things weigh, too."

"They do," said Cousin Willy. "And when they got them on top of the bank, they hauled up the carriages and the shot and the powder. And the Indians sat round complacently in the shade and watched them,—watched their land being taken away from them—"

This gave me an idea and I picked out a nice water-oak and made myself comfortable. I dozed off as they were emptying the last canoe and doling out the axes to shape the three-inch planks for the stockade. When

I came to, Cousin Willy had the guns mounted on the carriages but was having a terrible time getting them up the ramps to the terreplein; he had his coat off and his cuffs turned half way up his lean forearms.

At long last he seemed to get it in something like the shape he wanted and he made a final circuit of the ramparts. Then he put on his coat and we drove round to Dunavant's, where I bought him a Coca-Cola.

Having thus sprinkled what was practically holy water on our reunion, we parted, the colonel touching the knob of his stick to his hat brim as Ninety-eight, with that motorized flourish and roar which it is simply presumption for any pale-faced chauffeur to try to imitate, whisked him out into the traffic.

I frankly hardly expected ever to see Cousin Willy again, and if he was the Effingham my mother had been I doubt if he expected to see me. We in the South regard our kin more or less in the light of an Organized Reserves, to be called to the colors in an emergency like a marriage or a funeral, and even to undergo an occasional training period at a family-reunion barbecue, but for the most part the kinship is on inactive service and we not only rarely encounter each other directly but if we chance to pass on the street are as likely as not to fail in recognition.

I wasn't worried about him. He had hinted at building a garden, at raising roses and camellias, at even writing his memoirs, and I felt that with those things and now and then a hand of bridge or poker with his old chums, he would be able to pass his remaining years in a well-earned peace and contentment. I returned to my desk in the editorial rooms of the *Leader* (if I may give such a title to their simple squalor), being careful to drop no hint of Cousin Willy's return for fear Ella Sue might print it in "Society" and thus bring obloquy upon an otherwise respected name,—for one of the chief social objects of life in the South is to so manage our affairs that our name achieves a total eclipse from public print until the occasion of our final ceremony, at which time, if all has been handled well, like a swan, it sings at last in some glory from the top of Page One.

CHAPTER II

Now one warm morning a few weeks later, it must have been in May, Mr. Earl Hoats, with a somewhat reflective look nesting in his quarter-inch lenses, entered his office, hung up his hat and coat, and sat down at his desk. He had been talking very casually to Mr. Parish Goff, editor of the *Morning News,* and he leaned now over his desk to consider what he had learned, his shirt-sleeves on the glass covering a collection of those blithe sales-ladies mailed out monthly by the Valley Insurance Agency vividy illustrating the consequences of "Partial Coverage." Through the heavy smoke of his morning cigar, he gazed out, apparently at the folksy scene of the Dionne Quints decorating a wall calendar, but really at the immediate and not so immediate future of Earl Hoats, and it seemed to him that some aspects of the moment suggested the tide which, taken at the flood, led on to fortune, and that his future in general might be on the way to assuming a color and outline inferior only to those of the seductive emissaries of the Valley Insurance Agency.

The proper development of that future, he believed, hinged largely on whether or not the *Leader* came out in full-throated editorial support of that modest ordinance of the Aldermen which I had told him about, designed to change the name of "Monument Square" to "Toolen Square." From the conversation he had just had with the *News*, he was reasonably certain that its editorial pages were going to be extremely silent on the proposal, and for the *Leader* to rush into the breach and endorse it, might very possibly turn out to be the seed of a Municipal Building-Hoats combination destined to flower into Heaven knew what beauty.

That the *News* was planning to hold its peace was not owing to a more sensitive loyalty to either the Lost Cause itself or to local tradition, but simply to the fact that a frostiness had begun to coat the once-warm relations between Parish Goff and Mr. Doc Buden. The cause of this precipitation was that Mr. Goff, sharing a Mason-jar of corn whiskey with the manager of Mr. Buden's radio station, WFK, on a weekend fishing expedition in the Ogeechee Swamp, had picked up a breath-taking summary of the debit and credit sides of WFK's ledger, and Mr. Goff determined then and there, before leaving Ogeechee water, that if there was any way in which another radio station could be set up in Fredericksville, he was going to be the man to set it up. Mr. Buden, learning of this gratuitous offer to share the take, let it be known through appropriate channels that the prospect of two radio stations in a town the size of Fredericksville failed to arouse in him any great enthusiasm. But Mr. Goff, hopelessly seduced by WFK's credit balance, was determined to go ahead,—and a considerable frostiness appeared in the air.

Mr. Hoats felt that now was on the whole an auspicious moment to extend a friendly hand in the general direction of Mr. Doc Buden and the other members of that more or less exclusive fraternity headquartered in the Municipal Building. Though he had only recently been advanced to the office of Managing Editor, he had occupied the City Desk across the hall since he had been hurled into our midst nearly a decade ago and he was quite familiar with what it meant to a newspaper to be subject to the kindly thoughts of the brotherhood; indeed, it was, he at heart suspected, a failure to reach any such workable amity with the Home Folks Party that eventually caused the removal of his predecessor. Not that the owners of the *Leader*, high up in a skyscraper looking out into the breezes of Lake Michigan, had ever given the Fredericksville Municipal Building a second thought; their second thoughts, not to mention their first, were devoted exclusively to the red and black ink on the *Leader's* books, which they took to be quite a different matter. Mr. Hoats didn't take it that way; he had an idea that the color of the predominant ink on their books was a more or less reliable index of the felicity with which they were regarded at the Municipal Building. If that benignity, which had so long blessed the *News*, could now, by a judicious feeding of the tender sprouts of discord, be turned away from the other sheet and on to the *Leader*, the happy results might carry far beyond any possibility of at present visualizing them.

He scrutinized his cigar for a final moment, then set it decisively between his teeth and pressed the button that would summon his right-hand man, Dewey. Having made his decision, he turned, while waiting, to his morning mail.

. . . . In about a minute and a half, with what he felt unconsciously was a miraculous promptness for the portly Dewey, there was a firm knock on the door and it was pushed open. He went on to finish reading the letter before him, waving Dewey to draw up a chair.

He heard the chair being drawn up as he reached the end of the page. Then becoming suddenly conscious that something was amiss, indeed perhaps catching a glimpse of a towering height that could not belong to Dewey, he popped up his head and beheld what he later described as an almost overwhelming sight.

He had supposed he was quite used to the varied procession of human animals that wound like an old-time circus parade through the offices of any Southern newspaper, from evangelists and strayed cowboys to the lavender of Colonial Dames, but he thought he had never seen anything more improbable than the figure standing there before him.

In its details it was not so outlandish: a sinewy man in perhaps his middle sixties, his well-shaped head surmounted by the immaculate dome of a white pith helmet which he was in the act of removing. He carried under his left arm a neat walking stick, and on his left wrist, like a falcon, what Mr. Hoats's old reportorial eye noted as Osborn's "Naval Operations" Volume III, a long and tanned forefinger disappearing into the midst of its pages, the black binding sharp against the fine blue-and-white stripes of his fresh cotton jacket. Mr. Hoats observed the fact that for almost the first time in his life the removal of a hat that revealed the pink expanse of a totally bald cranium had in no way surprised him; indeed, he felt it would have been a shock if the man had not been bald.

It was not the details so much as the whole presence of the man. He didn't know quite how to express it, but there seemed to be somehow a greater certainty than usual that somebody had arrived there in the room with him.

The cumulative effect of the whole thing was to raise Mr. Hoats, awkwardly perhaps but no less positively, to his feet, a courtesy that he practically never bothered with. The truth was that, while, in the primitive superstitiousness of his unconscious, he was beginning to wonder whether this caller was an avenging messenger of Jehovah or even Jehovah himself, his practical experience came to the fore and he found himself deciding that though the chances were very much against his being Jehovah, they were not so great against his being the next thing to Him: either the president of the owning company from Lake Michigan or the chairman of its Board of Directors.—Into all of which uncertainties, his Ohio skepticism shot the hideous possibility that he might now be rising in greeting to some fabulous peddler.

"I am Colonel Effingham," said Cousin Willy gravely in the big round voice; "W. Seaborn Effingham, Colonel United States Army, retired."

"Good morning, Colonel," Mr. Hoats mumbled, extending his hand, feeling an exquisite relief at finding his visitor was something tangible and finite like a soldier; up to this point Cousin Willy had been about as bewildering to him as an unincarnated voice. "Take a chair," he added generously, settling more comfortably back into his own. "You are visiting in Fredericksville, Colonel?"

"Not at all," said Cousin Willy, laying his book and helmet on a corner of the desk but retaining the walking stick. "I was born in Fredericksville. My father and my grandfather and my great-grandfather were all born in Fredericksville. To an Effingham, Fredericksville is home."

"I see," Mr. Hoats granted him, patiently.

"My grandfather served four years in the Army of the West. He was at Perryville, at Shiloh, at Chickamauga, at Lookout Mountain. My father was too young to go; when Beauregard fired on Sumter he was only nine."

33

"That was a little young," said Mr. Hoats pleasantly, rearranging a copy pencil on his desk.

"My people are soldiers," Cousin Willy went on. "My great-grandfather fell at the gates of Mexico City. I was at Santiago; I was wounded at the beginning of the action at San Juan Hill. I was at the Siege of Panama."

"Siege of Panama?" said Mr. Hoats, digging frantically into his high school history books on what appeared to be the warm trail of fraud.

"For fifty years, Mr. Editor," Cousin Willy continued, "the forces of civilization, the brigades of progress, had been held at bay on the Isthmus, unable to advance into the jungle, unable to join the waters of the two great oceans. And do you know what blocked them? Gatlin guns? Minnie balls, grape, canister? Superior forces? Guerrilla bands?" Cousin Willy shook his head. Then he lifted his stick and lowered it at Mr. Hoats's flattening chest in somewhat the manner of Custer on the Big Horn; when the ferrule dropped to about the bottom of Mr. Hoats's left lung, Cousin Willy said, "Mosquitoes!"

Mr. Hoats didn't jump, but he did bat his eye. "Perhaps one of my boys could fix up a little story for Sunday," he began placatingly.

"*Anopheles maculipennis*," specified Cousin Willy, disdaining the offer. "*Stegomyia fasciata*. For half a century this enemy, less than a quarter of an inch in stature, had blocked the economic march of a nation of a hundred million people.—It was insupportable."

"Colonel," began Mr. Hoats, catching sight of Dewey beyond the glass of the door.

"We laid a siege on them," said Cousin Willy. He clasped the stick behind his back and continued, as though talking to a class of junior officers at the Army War College. "There are two great alternate methods of dislodging a fortified enemy: you may, one, force upon him what he does not want, or, two, you may deny him what he does want. You may, one, propel at him various substances unfriendly to his well-being, such as gas, fire, bits of metal, edged steel; or you may prevent his receiving various substances essential to his well-being, such as water, provisions, heat, oxygen. The particular tactical problem involved here, due to the highly specialized nature of the enemy, his size, his cover, his guerrilla methods, eliminated the first alternative. So we chose the second. We blockaded General Stegomyia; we cut him off from reinforcements, from essential war materials. We hammered his communications. We attacked his mobilization points by draining them; we sprayed his concentrations with oil; we screened his wells, we planted Fifth Columns of fish in the waters to attack his reservists and his ammunition dumps.—As you know, he abandoned his position with heavy losses and the American forces moved in—"

"You are back in Fredericksville for good now, Colonel?" said Mr. Hoats with an unconscious note of plaintiveness in his voice, wiggling a forefinger with elaborate unconcern at Dewey oblivious beyond the glass door.

Cousin Willy paid no more attention to the interruption than if it had been a bugle call belonging to another regiment. In fact his whole attitude toward Mr. Hoats was that of a humanitarian toward some creature like, say, a grasshopper or a cricket. He couldn't even remember Mr. Hoats's name,—and moreover, didn't seem to give the matter a second thought. He appeared to consider "Mr. Editor" entirely adequate and let it go at that.

He took Mr. Editor across the Isthmus with Goethals, presented him to a Captain Hickock at the great Miraflores Locks, handed him a ringside seat at the ceremony of joining the waters; he took him back to Cuba, to the foot of San Juan Hill, stretched him out half naked under a tropical sun, took him at the double a few meters up the slope, shot him in the left thigh just as Spain was abandoning her position on the crest, propped him up on one elbow waving his men on with a sweat-soaked campaign hat—

At this point Dewey, having at last got his signal, entered the office, and Cousin Willy cut himself short with the disheartening promise, "But more of all that another day.—What I am leading up to, Mr. Editor, is the possibility of a column of war commentary in your paper."

"I've thought of that, Colonel. I've even communicated with some of the syndicates about it. Those things are expensive, though, and we are just a small paper; we don't have much money to put—"

"You don't understand me. I will write your war commentary."

This almost took what breath Mr. Hoats had left from the Cuban campaign; when what he needed most was Cousin Willy's absence, the sudden alternative of having him permanently on the payroll was like adding sunstroke to his shattered thigh.

He shook his head exhaustedly. "We couldn't pay you enough, Colonel, to make it worth your while. I can get a syndicated column for three or four dollars a week, and I can't even afford that—"

"Hell's flood, sir! I don't want pay."

Mr. Hoats's pale cheeks grew noticeably paler under the impact of this proposition. It looked like something-for-nothing, which was a banshee that he was tough enough to know did not exist in this life; whether or not a laborer was worthy of his hire, you always had, in one way or another, to hire him. If you accepted something for nothing, you were only buying an item without knowing what you were going to pay for it.

He rocked back in his chair and smiled loftily for a few seconds, trying to give his mind a moment in which to grasp the potentialities of the bill. He finally called for an armistice by suggesting that Cousin Willy allow him a day or two in which to consider this generous and civic-minded offer. "How can I get in touch with you, Colonel?"

Cousin Willy accepted the truce, gave him his telephone number, picked up his book and his helmet, and without more ado, saluted him in a gracious good-bye, and departed.

Mr. Hoats cast after him a heart-felt sigh of relief. "For God's sake, Dewey!"

Dewey shook his head sympathetically.

"Who is that guy, Dewey?"

"Never saw him before."

"Find out. I don't want his pedigree and I don't want his military history; I've got all that. I want to know what he's doing in Fredericksville." He paused to relight his long-expired cigar, puffing at the acrid fumes with an expression of excruciating pain. "And what we've done to deserve it. I want to know the name of the last lunatic asylum he attended—"

"Was he offering us a war column?"

"Yes, free for nothing.—What do you think?"

"Well, boss, when something comes to you sitting on top of a silver platter—"

"I know; there's a string tied to it on the other side."

"I wasn't going to say that. I'm not sure this old guy knows how to tie a string."

"Well, Dewey, suppose everything has just gone completely haywire in Fredericksville like it has everywhere else in the world and there's no string tied to it. Do you think it would make a good feature?"

"It wouldn't be like taking on another comic—"

"A comic costs money, Dewey. We might get this thing for a smile,—maybe less."

"If we wanted to cancel the Washington column, we could save—"

"Look into it, Dewey. If there's a string, find it.—

Now there was something I wanted to talk to you about," he went on, turning his spectacles at the far ceiling. "It's gone. I can't think of it.—I'll call you later, if it hasn't been knocked out of my head for ever."

Dewey waited a second, administering what psychological first aid he could, then got up and started to the door.

As he moved, however, Mr. Hoats's eye chanced to fall on the glass covering of his desk and the lines of a cheerful blonde guilelessly sliding down some banisters without any shirt on and he recalled once more the inspiring shape of his future as he had seen it earlier in the morning; he snapped his fingers at Dewey and waved him back into the chair. "Dewey, I want an editorial for Sunday on old Pud Toolen—"

"Pud's been dead—"

"Dig him up. Civic-leader angle, what he did for the city—"

Dewey muttered, "For or to?" but Mr. Hoats paid no attention.

"End it off on the note that the *Leader* takes pride, pardonable pride, in joining its voice to the clamor for naming the square in the center of Broad Street for this civic-minded benefactor. The time has come in

40

the growth and expansion of our city when it is no longer tolerable that its principal square should continue without a name, a name looking to the future not to the past,—and so forth. You know, Dewey; give it the works. Let me see before you set it, I may want to add something."

2

When Dewey came in I was at my desk hammering out a little four-inch story for Page Two about the election for a vacant seat on the Board of Aldermen being called off because no one would offer his head in opposition to the Home Folks candidate. Leroy, our Police-Fire man, was reading the comics in the exchanges, and Ella Sue was in her bower probably turning out her weekly sedative for those stricken with love.

"Anybody," said Dewey, looking at a piece of paper, "ever hear of an old guy named W. Seaborn Effingham?"

I jumped two letters and a space.

Ella Sue shook her head, Leroy came out from behind Moon Mullins and went back again.

"What's he done?" I said tentatively.

"Know him?"

"I know the name."

He sat down on a corner of my desk and told me what Cousin Willy had offered to do.

I tried not to show it, but there's no use denying that it upset me a good deal. You see, it was one thing for me, young (that is, I was twenty-eight), ambitious, headed in time perhaps for the dizzy heights of the City Desk and a clean thirty-five a week, throwing off a mystery for the pulps now and then, and nursing in the back of my head, as a good Baptist nurses the vision of an overstuffed bench beside the Judgment Seat, the idea of some day writing a full-length novel that would land me among the angels in Hollywood, —it was one thing for me to write for the paper, but it was quite something else for Cousin Willy to do it. And anyway, what I wrote wasn't signed; it didn't involve any complications of name and family. Cousin Willy's proposition meant a signature and though this would be "Effingham" and not "Marbury," still everybody knew the Effinghams were mixed up with the Marburys and both sides of the family would suffer.

I didn't know what Cousin Willy was thinking about. Either he had been out of the South for so long he had become negligent about this sort of thing, or else he may have felt that there were so few Effinghams

42

now living in Fredericksville it didn't matter (the only one I knew of was old Cousin Albert who was as far removed from us genealogically as his grocery store in the neighborhood of the colored cemetery was from the heart of town). Also, however, there was the even more disturbing fact that there was undoubtedly something slightly rampant about Cousin Willy; what if he might just not care, anyhow?

Of course, at that moment Mr. Hoats had not agreed to run the column; but considering that Cousin Willy had offered to do it for nothing, I felt that Mr. Hoats's resistance had already been so undermined as to be no longer worth counting on. Cousin Willy might not know it yet, but I thought the truth of the matter was that he was hired. The only catch was the possibility of that string, and I didn't think it stood much chance of holding against the weight of what was really, from the point of view of the editor of a small paper, a fairly attractive offer.

"I don't know how much experience he has had with writing," I mentioned, with a slight stiffness in my professional neck.

"Anybody can write," Dewey began vehemently, when the telephone rang and the dice were cast.

"One column twice a week on the editorial page,"

said Mr. Hoats. "Call it '*On the Firing Line*,' thirty-six point Bodoni. Sign it 'W. Seaborn Effingham, Col., U. S. Army, retired,' spell 'retired' lower case. Inset a one-inch cut of the colonel showing the collar of his uniform. Build it up two or three days before you start. Get some informal shots of the author at work and play—"

"I'll do it," I said. I had visions of Leroy or Ella Sue going out there and Cousin Willy asking if they knew his kinsman, Albert Marbury. "I can make the pictures too."

"You better take Ella Sue along to handle the story—"

"Let me have it, Dewey. Let me handle it all. Two of us like that would make him nervous—"

"Two of us never made him nervous this morning."

"Let me have it. Give me a break—"

"Okie," said Dewey. "It's yours."

3

I waited until the next morning on account of the light; the shot I saw was an angle up at Cousin Willy on the Confederate breastworks with a weather eye open for Sherman coming over the ridge, and the afternoon sun wouldn't do it.

Truth to tell, I was a little anxious about the column. As long as an Effingham was going to do it, I wanted to see it a success and I was somewhat at a loss as to how we could establish that necessary sympathetic contact with his readers. Something had to be found to quiet our subscribers' spontaneous distrust of a stranger, to establish some sort of bond, "reader confidence" is our phrase. I thought maybe the Confederate War might do it. I was afraid that in spite of his familiar name and in spite of anything I could say in the story, our readers were going to feel he was a foreigner, whose point of view had little connection with theirs.

And of course, in this, up to a certain point, they would be quite correct,—up to the point at which Colonel Effingham left off and Cousin Willy began. Colonel Effingham's outlook was entirely different from theirs, based on a lifetime's detachment from civil problems, on a deep-rooted habit of authority, and, probably most telling of all, on the fact that his present financial status was as immutable as the Pension Bureau of the United States Government. I didn't

45

know whether we could overcome all that or not. I thought perhaps that standing on the earthworks of a common past might possibly bring out Cousin Willy, who I felt was so Southern as to be almost typical. Allowing for being mistaken about him on such short acquaintance, I tentatively pictured him as an exceedingly simple man, with an inherent romanticism that tended to cast a sort of formalism and perhaps pompousness over an attitude essentially direct and guileless. However appealing the quality of what Colonel Effingham wrote, I felt that a crash could be avoided only by Cousin Willy. So it was Cousin Willy I set out to photograph.

"How you-all getting on, Ninety-eight?" I said to Ninety-eight, who had walked toward me through the dim hall from the back porch, already in as easy possession of Cousin Willy's stride as one day he would be of his shirts and pants.

"Doing nicely, thank you, Mr. Al."

I told him I should like to see the colonel and he said he thought it would be all right because the colonel hadn't started to work yet; he glanced at the open door into the office. "Now if 'at door was shut," he smiled and shook his head.

I waited for a minute on the back porch while

46

Ninety-eight went to find Cousin Willy. The garrison seemed to be in pretty good shape; I could hear Cousin Emma's voice twittering pleasantly off in the kitchen wing, and I noticed that the porch had been painted in a sort of yellow-and-white combination that I had seen once on the officers quarters at a Coast Artillery post. My eye fell on a bulletin board under a glass frame fastened on the wall between the kitchen and the back door; there was a typewritten sheet on it giving the times of meals, another that looked off-hand like a menu, as well as a planting calendar from a garden magazine and a recipe for "*Shrimp Canal Zone.*"

"Them's the Orders of the Day," Ninety-eight explained, returning. Then he drew himself up sharply and delivered his message: "The colonel presents his compliments, sir, and says will you kindly join him at the redoubt."

I found Cousin Willy strolling near the earthworks, a faded khaki shirt unbuttoned at the neck, smoking a pipe the like of which I had not seen since the days of metal lamp shades fitted with colored glass; the curve in it wasn't just a curve, it was a hairpin turn, and the bowl, which looked as if it might have held a 35-mm film cartridge, rested on his newly-shaved chin. I guess it was what used to be called a bulldog pipe, though the

47

last time I had seen one was at recess in grammar school when an Italian organ grinder tossed it to a small and bewildered monkey.

Yet this morning it was a hale sort of thing, somehow; and halely the colonel smoked it, now and then pressing the coal down with a tough first finger. It struck me that he seemed to take the same sort of quiet pride in the particular individuality he had raised as a nurseryman in a new variety of camellia.

"I didn't know you were planning to join the great fraternity of newspapermen," I said with that sort of banter we Southerners, like a man on base, never intend to get caught very far away from, as he gripped my hand in his big palm.

He smiled a little. "A paper ought to publish some sort of war commentary nowadays, mine or somebody else's. A newspaper is run for the good of the community, isn't it?"

"Well, anyhow," I said, not wishing to rush into this treacherous jungle so early in the morning, "I am glad you came to the *Leader* instead of going round the corner." (That was our customary way of referring to the *News* which, as far as we were officially concerned, was without father or name.) We got a good deal of fun for a minute or two out of having, as

48

he put it, a "common boss,"—his a wholesome pleasure, mine discreetly vindictive.

"Cousin Willy," I said, getting down to business, "we want an interview and we want some pictures, two or three informal shots to run along with the advance build-up. It looks like they are planning to put you over in a big way."

I had thought I might have trouble in persuading him to let me make the pictures, but not at all; he didn't seem to give it any more thought than signing his name.

I made two or three shots against the fortifications, but they weren't quite what we needed. They hadn't much warmth, hadn't much to demand that bond of reader confidence. I felt there was some slight hope for them because of the bulldog pipe,—but nothing like the hope, I suddenly realized, there would have been if I could have stirred up the bulldog himself—

"You haven't by any chance got a dog round here, have you, sir?"

"What do you want with a dog?" he smiled.

I just told him dogs made good pictures.

"Ninety-eight may know a dog," he said indulgently. "Oh, orderly!"

When Ninety-eight appeared on the double, Cousin

49

Willy said to him, "Orderly, is there a dog on the post? Our guest here wants a dog. It is not up to us to question his motives but merely to fulfill his desires as well as we can—"

"I just want to take his picture," I said.

"There's old Buck, Colonel," Ninety-eight suggested.

"I don't know him," said Cousin Willy.

"Lives down yonder in the hollow."

"Well, have him report up here immediately—"

Then things suddenly began to click. All at once everything seemed to fall in line. The only detail that went wrong was that, in my excitement, I dropped the yellow filter and lost a cloud backdrop, but it is possible that even there it was all right, our presses having been second-hand in 1906 and having no love for cloud effects. I knocked off the lens shade, but I don't think that made much difference—

Ninety-eight whistled up a great black-and-white pointer from down in the pines somewhere and the creature came bounding up the hill like a good-natured antelope; it passed me without so much as turning a nostril, leaped with a long elasticity up on the old Confederate bastion where Cousin Willy had preceded me and pulled up in the tall grass beside him, shaking the weeds with a resilient tail and gazing off, as if instinctively, in the direction of the road by which General Sherman had all but come. It was here that I knocked the lens shade off the camera; but I shot anyway,—the colonel bareheaded on top of the mound, the pipe on his chin, the faithful canine beside him, all against a sky.

. . . . It was a honey. It had reader-confidence written all over it. When I laid it on Mr. Hoats's desk he even snapped his fingers. "What's his name?"

"Colonel W. Seaborn—"

"The dog!"

"Buck."

Mr. Hoats shook his head. Then in a minute, with that instinctive grasp of the situation that made him the newsman he was, he said, "His name's Rover," and he wrote it on the back of the damp print.

He was so pleased I thought the vision even crossed his spectacles of reducing my salary and making me the regular photographer.

But if he considered it, he didn't act on it promptly enough, because it wasn't many weeks later that the reader-confidence in that picture began to backfire at us and I was almost ready to swear I had never heard the expression.

51

CHAPTER III

WELL, we built up Cousin Willy like a motion picture the producers have lost faith in. By the time his first column appeared there was hardly anybody in town who had not heard of Colonel Effingham and his faithful dog, Rover. Our subscribers seemed to open their arms to the pair,—as a general thing, though there were some, mostly among the long-term-paid-in-advance group, who were bewildered if not even dismayed at this apparent want of modesty on the part of an Effingham.

Among these, of course, were Cousin Willy's personal friends; they were, on the whole, not happy about it. They seemed to have a feeling that somehow somebody was tampering with the flag, or, to put it on a basis of neckties, that somebody had simply reached over and flicked the school tie out of their composite waistcoat.

Of course, you understand, I was a sort of poor relation of Cousin Willy's. My father had been a doctor, one of those family physicians of olden times who never sent bills to his friends and who had too many friends; he collected books and played occasionally in an inconsequential way upon a wooden flute. The result of all this was that I inherited a somewhat ill-balanced but eloquent library and a musical instrument, but not much else except such a poor opinion of the earning powers of medicine that I took up journalism. I mean to say, our branch of the family had very little connection with the world of trade and money; the local bank presidents and captains of industry were little more to us than names of people of a mildly inherent enmity, like policemen; I knew Mr. Clyde Manadue and Mr. Bibb and Mr. Sterling Tignor but they didn't know me. I was merely "the *Leader* reporter," and the fact that my father might very likely, in bygone days, have serenaded some convalescent member of their household did not serve to bring us any closer now.

With Cousin Willy, though, it was different; of course he was more nearly their age, but more important than that was the fact that the Effinghams had been Cotton Row people in the days when cotton was cotton. He had been out of touch with them for many years, but the root of the old school friendship was as green as ever and when he returned they more or less held out both hands to him,—held them out partly to the old friend but particularly to the old soldier. To us in the South, long nurtured in arms, a friend is a friend but a soldier is a hero; a headstone may mark the resting place of a pal, but a shaft of Georgia marble commemorates the brave.

Cousin Willy, then, was much in demand at the more substantial tables of Fredericksville; he could talk old times with them, "billygoat days," or he could expatiate to them on the strategy and tactics of the war. In addition to that, he could hold his own at the average bridge meeting and he knew to a mathematical certainty the Saturday afternoon chances of filling an inside straight.

The principal one of these tables was that of his old chum from Habersham Academy days, Clyde Manadue,—once first-class private in Corporal Effingham's squad, now president and owner of the controlling stock of the Southeastern Fertilizer Company, with an office on Cotton Row and a mixing plant built with some sagacity on a spur of the Georgia-Carolina Railroad at the exact point where the city ended and Habersham County began.

In 1898, when he built the original plant, the site was mutually satisfactory to him and to His Honor, Mayor Pud Toolen; being across the city line, it complied with Section 17-B, Paragraph 9, of the Building Code which forbade the erection of structures for the manufacture or mixing of commercial fertilizers within the city limits, and being within six inches of the line, it made possible a no-insignificant saving in insurance premiums on account of Mayor Toolen's fire plug located opposite the entrance.

The only drawback to the site was one that had been almost impossible to foresee. Mr. Manadue, being by nature, even in his youth, conservative in his outlook, made adequate provision for the probability of rainy days but neglected almost altogether to allow for the possibility of bright ones, and it was bright ones that after a while began to appear. For with the slow depletion of the Georgia topsoil by the ravenous cotton plant, it became more and more obvious as the years rolled by that the only way a man could raise cotton in that trade area was by the liberal use of fertilizer; and since the personal prestige of a farmer required that he raise as much cotton as his furrows would hold, Mr. Clyde was before long faced with the necessity of expanding his factory.

He was not wholly unprepared for the first expansion. His plot of land was roughly triangular in shape, bounded by the city and the railroad and a broad slow creek that served as overflow to the canal system of the town, and he had room for new buildings at the back toward the point where the tracks crossed the creek. Beyond that, of course he could not go, but in 1907 when he built the new mixing sheds, what worried him was not the possibility of ever having need of more space but what seemed to him the appalling imminence of not needing what he had.

But the surface of Georgia, under the unremitting attacks of rain and cotton, continued to be transported to the Atlantic down the copper-colored Savannah and to decline both in quantity and in quality, and the first thing he knew he was being cramped again. It did not seem particularly serious, however; true he had gone as far as he could in two directions but the city line at this point was hardly distinguishable to the uninitiated, both city and county here consisting largely of bare fields and railroad sidings and discarded wooden passenger coaches jacked up on blocks for the use of track crews and watchmen, and the only thing standing between him and expansion into the city was, in cold reality, a nod from Mr. Pud Toolen.

To picture this line as inviolable required a kind of imagination that Mr. Manadue, even in his flightiest days, did not have. So he put in a call for the livery stable of Mr. Pud Toolen's son-in-law, from a rocking chair in the broad door of which Mr. Toolen now administered the affairs of the district, and asked him if he would step round to Cotton Row sometime during the morning.

Mr. Toolen stepped round and they talked it over, Mr. Clyde in stiff linen, Mr. Toolen in corpulent black. A scheme was readily worked out by which Mr. Clyde might build certain necessary storage sheds across the line in the city and build his new mixers on the site of the old storage sheds. Conducting Mr. Toolen to the door, Mr. Clyde remarked with a not-to-change-the-subject air, that he had been wanting for some time past to send Mr. Toolen a little contribution to his charities and he hoped Mr. Toolen would see fit to accept a small check he would be sending round to him in a day or two. "Make it out to cash, please, sir," said Mr. Toolen, and the interview came to a congenial close.

That was many years ago, of course; I dare say Mr. Clyde never laid eyes on Mr. Pud Toolen again, or certainly not both eyes. It was a little like your relationship to the undertaker; while you might not exactly cultivate his acquaintance, you also realized that it was folly to stir up the antagonism of someone who usually came in handy before all was said and done. The least Mr. Clyde could do would have been to park his car, while he was at the office, in the livery stable that before long was renovated into a garage, but he didn't even do that. It wasn't possible, of course, to forget Mr. Toolen, but he did seem to overlook him, —though, among the towering banks of flowers at Mr. Toolen's funeral, Mr. Hoats's ready eye was pleased to note a considerable wreath from the Southeastern Fertilizer Company.

As I say, Cousin Willy came in for a good deal of merry kidding from Mr. Manadue on account of the build-up we gave him, "this old publicity hound," and that sort of thing. The word "photogenic" had descended upon us at about that time and Cousin Willy was allowed to feel the full weight of it,—all in good humor, you know (as Mr. Manadue once said to him, with a sotto voce hand on his shoulder, "We're right behind you, Will"), and yet having an almost impalpa-

58

ble bite to it too, from the fact, as I have pointed out, that he had stepped a little closer to the footlights than the Fredericksville tradition gave any precedent for.

The banter didn't bother Cousin Willy; in fact, I think he rather enjoyed it. To be stopped on Broad Street and kidded a little bit was a novel and on the whole grateful relief after a lifetime spent under the chilly greeting of the military salute. It didn't seem to divert him from his decision to do the column for us any more than two or three pine saplings would divert the course of a resolute tank.

. . . . One of his early columns surprised us by departing from the war in Europe and going back to pick up a conversation in the winter of 1735 between General Oglethorpe and one Mr. Ken O'Brien. The watchful Dewey took the copy across to Mr. Hoats, who ran through it.

"What's the trouble with it, Dewey?"

"I thought we were printing a war commentary—"

"Listen, Dewey. The war is in Europe, General Oglethorpe is a local boy—"

"I just wanted you to check it."

"The way to get the most out of a feature like this is to give the guy his head—"

Dewey put it on the hook.

Cousin Willy described how Mr. Ken O'Brien, paddling meditatively down the river on his way to Charles Town, his canoe piled high with beaver and deerskins to be exchanged for "blankets, guns, powder, salt, kettles, beads, hoes, axes, and no doubt, West Indies rum," was signalled from the bank by a sentry in a red coat. Mr. O'Brien beached his boat on the sand at the bottom of Yamacraw Bluff and, obeying orders, climbed the long ladder to the top where General Oglethorpe, "an earnest young man of thirty-nine," was sitting on the great trunk of a newly-felled pine tree waiting for him.

" 'The reason I stopped you,' said General Oglethorpe, taking a silver snuff-box out from under his plaid (for he wore the Highland habit), and seating Mr. O'Brien, with a wave of his stick, on the log at a reasonable distance (it was winter and perfectly apparent that Mr. O'Brien bathed predominantly in the summer), 'is that, now that I have established my two fortified points on the coast south of here to keep an eye on the Papists, I am considering planting a defensive position up in your neighborhood. I understand there's already a trading post up there on the Carolina side.'

" 'Yes, sir,' said Mr. O'Brien, 'and we have a little camp on the Georgia side too.'

" 'That's what I hear,' said General Oglethorpe.

" 'Most of the trade is with the Georgia tribes and we have a little camp there where one or two of us— well—'

" 'Where one or two of you sort of jump the gun, is that it?'

" 'Well, not exactly, sir—'

" 'However that may be,' said General Oglethorpe, 'it doesn't make sense to me that our Georgia Indians, bringing in the skins of Georgia deer and Georgia buffalo, should turn them over for the profit of Carolina. After all, these Carolinians have put us in a pretty tight spot here, keeping the Catholics out of Charles Town for them, and I don't see how they can reasonably expect us to hand them a lot of our valuable deer- skins into the bargain. I don't see why that profit doesn't rightly belong to Georgia,—and frankly, O'Brien,' the general shook his head, 'from the showing my people have put up so far, I think we are going to need all the profit we can lay our hands on.'

" 'I've heard they don't like to work,' said Mr. O'Brien sympathetically.

61

" 'They seem to think,' General Oglethorpe specified, 'that because I got them out of debt once, there's
no reason I shouldn't get them out again. I've given
every man fifty acres and all his farming equipment,
and now they want me to bring them a boatload of
blackamoors to work the equipment. It looks sometimes like the more you do for some people, the more
they expect.' The general gazed out across the sunny
marshes for a minute, struggling with his discourage-
ment; then he changed his tone and got down to business: 'But what I had in mind about this post up the
river was, I want a good clear view up and down the
bank for at least a mile. I intend to give these redskins
a fair deal, but after all it will be my idea of a fair deal,
not theirs, and there's no use having a bend in the
river where you can't see what they're doing.'

" 'I think you're right—'

" 'You know Tomochichi?'

" 'Not to speak to, no, sir.'

" 'Tomochichi wants me to do some price fixing.'

" 'That's mighty touchy business, meddling with
prices, General,' Mr. O'Brien said wistfully.

" 'I know it is, but these are touchy times. He wants
me to set up a scale,—ten buckskins, one gun; five

buckskins, one pistol, and so on down the line. Because as it is now, some people take advantage of the Indians.'

"Mr. O'Brien lowered his eyes.

" 'I'm not thinking of you particularly,' said General Oglethorpe, 'but it's got to stop. I don't mind taking these people's lands; I'm a soldier and that's my business. But if you're going to buy something, it's cheaper in the long run to make a fair profit year in, year out, than to make a fortune one year and get shot in the head in an Indian war the next.'

"Mr. O'Brien nodded without much enthusiasm.

" 'Now this is going to mean a lot of work. Setting up a fort in this Georgia wilderness is no picnic. I'll want a fourteen-foot ditch, and I'll want a twelve-foot counterscarp of three-inch timber. I'll want a terreplein that will accommodate eight eighteen-pounders and there will have to be quarters and barracks for thirty-two officers and men—'

" 'You're really planning to take over, General.'

" 'I am,' said General Oglethorpe. 'This will be an important outpost of civilization and I intend to defend it as such. It is going to cost a lot of hard work, mean a lot of sacrifice. It's going to take a lot of courage;

but you can't build anything in this world without courage. Fortunately, though, we've got plenty of courage.—Are you married, O'Brien?'

" 'Well, sir—'

" 'I'll straighten that out for you when I get there. It's better to have marriage on a yes-and-no basis.— How many children have you got?'

" 'I've got about fourteen—'

" 'They'll all have the King's protection. Their fortunes will be the fortunes of Fort Frederick.—Go on to Charles Town and stop in on your way back. I'll have everything ready by then and I want you to guide us up the river—' "

. . . . That was the sort of thing it was and on the whole Mr. Hoats rather liked the local angle.

2

One morning round at the Municipal Building, after we had been running the column for a couple of weeks, Mr. Doc Buden beckoned me over to a corner of the Sheriff's Office and asked me what it was all about, listening as curiously as if he had been counting the pings on the cash register in the hotel barber shop. They were all still a little skeptical about the *Leader*, apparently not being quite convinced of the validity of Mr. Hoats's repentance and his assurances that a new leaf was in process of being turned.

I told him it was just a new war feature we had picked up locally.

"Don't know any Colonel Effingham."

"Nice fellow," I said. "His people come from round here."

"Like to meet him. Bring him around sometime."

"I sure will, Doc," I said, cringing a little.

"Yeah, bring him around. We like to meet new people. What ward's he live in?"

I told him I thought he lived in the county. We talked for a while, leaning our elbows here and there, watching the people who came in and out of the building, Mr. Buden lifting a right hand to practically everybody. He seemed to be in a good humor and as I was about to leave I mentioned the Toolen memorial to him. "Has anything more been done," I said, "about changing the name of the square?"

"You mean about naming the square.—It's in caucus now. Probably be presented to the Board next week."

"You reckon I could see a copy of the resolution before it goes to the Board?" I said.

Mr. Buden didn't move the elbow he was occupying, but with his free hand he waved at Mr. Mit Thurtig, who pushed his green eyeshade up to the top of his forehead and came over. He told Mit to see if he could find him a copy of the Toolen Memorial Resolution.

I watched him in admiration; he handled the thing as dextrously as he used to strop a razor.

"How does Earl feel about it all?" he said.

"Of course," I explained, "I can't speak for the editorial policy of the paper. I'm just a reporter. But it's my understanding Earl is all for it. Dewey told me he was fixing up a nice editorial about Mr. Pud."

"Looks like Earl's going to do all right on that paper."

I told him Earl was a good newspaperman.

Mit brought him an onion-skin copy of the resolution done up in a blue binding; he glanced at it and handed it to me. "Read it out," he said.

I read it to him. It was dressed up like Ninety-eight on his Sunday off; it was decorated with five "Whereas's," a "Now Therefore" and a "Furthermore." "Whereas the death of Earnest J. Toolen, April 5, 1931, had deprived the community of Fredericksville of one of its most beloved, patriotic and unselfish civil

66

servants, and Whereas it was a custom for said community to pay just tribute to its honored dead in a manner fitting and suitable" and so forth and so forth, and "Whereas the square in the center of the thoroughfare known as 'Broad Street' is now without a name" and so forth, and Whereas this and Whereas that, "Now Therefore be it resolved that the square hereinbefore particularized be called" and so forth, and that "suitable markers be erected to so designate the said square, and Furthermore that a bronze tablet bearing a memorial inscription hereinafter set forth in detail be placed in an appropriate spot in the said square and that what maps, charts, diagrams, plots and plans soever now in possession of the Board of Aldermen be altered to conform with this designation—"

"That's telling them, isn't it?" he said.

"That's undoubtedly telling them," I said.

He held out his hand for the paper.

"You don't want me just to keep this copy," I said, "until the Board passes it?"

"It might get printed too soon."

"Now, Doc," I said, "you know me better than that."

He patted me good-naturedly on the shoulder,—

but he kept the resolution. "You can tell Earl what's in it. But don't print anything about it until it goes through."

I jabbed the front of my hat upward in a way I had learned to do: "What's the matter, Doc, you scared the Board won't pass it?"

It being my joke, I laughed at it more than Mr. Buden, but we both enjoyed it and parted good friends. He had always been very nice to me, personally, but now that there was some evidence that Mr. Hoats was going to "get right," as we say, there seemed to be a slight change in the atmosphere between Mr. Doc Buden and me that reminded me of the Sunday when my father told the pastor of the Presbyterian Church that I was going to join the flock; a warmer light spread over the minister's face and the cordiality began to glow in his eyes like a blacksmith's smoldering coals under the pull of the bellows. And there was irresistibly a response in me, both then and now; I am practically helpless in the face of kindness and I went down the steps of the Municipal Building suffused with a curious contentment. How much of this was owing to the prospect of a change in those monotonous figures on my pay check which Mr. Hoats had hinted at, and how much to the more spiritual pleasure of seeing the door of the Sanctum cracked before me, I can't say; a considerable part of me, I dare say, responded to each.

However, with the exception of this commercially pretty non-negotiable warmth round my heart, I returned to the office with nothing to show for my morning. Nobody at the moment was in the outer office except the colored boy, Rucker, dabbing with a wizened broom round the feet of the desks; in the Society Office Ella Sue was sitting behind a typewriter flanked by a fistful of flowers in a drinking glass, considerably more of a decoration, I was sorry to admit, than the flowers. (We resented Miss Dozier, frankly, to about the extent a soldier of the line resents a headquarters clerk.) She was smoking a cigarette, looking at her window.

"Well," I called, as patronizingly as possible, "what's Society doing?"

She glanced out at me and gave her head a little backward jerk; I fumbled for my cigarettes and started across the office.

Then I heard a deep voice in her room and forgot the cigarettes; the next thing I knew she was saying, "Colonel, I want you to meet Mr. Marbury, one of our galaxy of star reporters—"

"Hello, my boy," said Cousin Willy, holding out

69

his hand from where he was sitting. "I've known Albert since he was no taller than a saber."

"How's the war going, Colonel?" I said. I sat down and we talked about it for a while and about dictatorships. We all got pretty worked up about dictatorships.

But dictatorships were a long way off and my little piece of news was burning a hole in my tongue. "I saw the resolution this morning," I told Ella Sue the first chance I got.

"Toolen Square," said Ella Sue with a wry smile, as if trying the sound of it.

"It's all set."

"What resolution, Albert?" said Cousin Willy.

"On the absolute QT, sir," I said, "the authorities are going to change the name of the square. You remember old Pud Toolen."

"I never heard of him."

"He used to be boss round here, Colonel. He ran things for us for twenty years—"

"Mayor for twenty years!"

"He was the mayors' boss for twenty years."

"But, Albert, the Citizens are the mayor's only boss." (His voice always seemed to pronounce "citizen" with a capital letter.)

"Political boss," I explained.

"I've heard the term," said Cousin Willy with a glance at Ella Sue as if to see whether she had, "but where do the Citizens come in?"

"Well, anyway," I said, not quite sure but that Cousin Willy was pulling my leg, "this one is getting a square named after him."

"I'm surprised we have any unnamed squares, Albert."

"Well, Colonel," I said, a little sorry I had got into all this, "yes, sir, and no, sir—"

"What square are they going to name after him?"

I took a long pull on my cigarette and told him.

He sat up straight: "Monument Square!"

"Apparently it has never had an official—"

"But they can't make a memorial to our Confederate dead into a memorial to their 'boss,' as you call him."

"Oh, yes they can," I laughed, though you couldn't help sort of admiring his indignation; there would be other indignation in town but it would reach expression only in the bosom of families. A few might mention it to me,—and I would hush them up, as usual, with my magic advice, "Why don't you write a letter to the paper?" Which was about like asking them why they didn't lie down on the railroad track in front of the Atlanta train.

"There's something about this," said the colonel, "that has a familiar ring to me." He walked over to the window and searched for it a moment in the junkyard below, then came back and sat down again. "I don't see where I could have run into anything like this in the service, but, still, it sort of reminds me, for some reason or other, of the Canal Zone—"

He seemed about to wander off into the maudlin reminiscences I have always associated with age, and I was glad when he gave it up and returned to the present. "The newspapers can prevent it," he said with a sudden brightness, innocent as a wild azalea.

I smiled at Ella Sue, who had been with us long enough to appreciate such humor. But she wasn't smiling.

"Does Mr. What's-his-name know about this?"

"I couldn't speak on that, sir," I said. "The information is not public yet."

"Well," said Cousin Willy, getting to his feet with a shove of his walking stick, "let's go tell him."

This took some of my breath away. Not that there was anything really surprising in somebody wanting to speak to the editor on such a subject; that happened now and then, though invariably on a don't-quote-me basis. It was the suddenness of it, and the fact that the story was not official yet, and the fact that my own participation was called for, and also the fact that the conviction was rapidly dawning on me that I had been talking too much.

"I've got a story to write," I said with tears in my voice; "I can't go now." I glanced at Ella Sue for help; women can always whip up a better excuse than men.

Ella Sue looked at me quite solemnly, no twinkle or anything: "Go ahead," she said. "It won't take you a minute."

I couldn't help laughing; Ella Sue could get the devil in her sometimes. "Wait a minute, Colonel," I said, "while I run over and see if he's in his office."

But Ella Sue didn't seem to trust me. "Ridiculous," she said; "I'll call him right here." And she picked up her phone and punched the editor's button.

It made me pretty mad for Society to try to put a news reporter on the spot. The trouble was I didn't know whether she was trying to be funny or whether she hadn't heard about the editorial Mr. Hoats had told Dewey to write,—or whether she was honestly simple enough to think the *Leader* might support Cousin Willy.

"Is Mr. Hoats in his office?" she said into the phone, while I took a painful turn to the window and the colonel stood there in front of her desk watching her. Then she broke the connection. "He's out of town."

"That's too bad," I said.

"Well, there must be a Second in Command," said Cousin Willy.

I told him there was no hurry about it. "It won't come up until next week, at the earliest. Next time you're in town, Colonel, why don't you just stop by and have a chat with Mr. Hoats. I know he'll be glad to do everything he can."

"It isn't a question of doing everything he can, Albert. It's a matter of repelling an assault in force."

"He's the man to see," I said. "And if you don't mind, just say you heard it; don't say I told you because, you see—"

"Don't quote me," Ella Sue muttered, as outright disagreeable as anybody could be.

I don't know whether this reminded me of the letter-to-the-paper gag or not, but something did. "Why don't you write a letter to the paper, Colonel?"

Cousin Willy looked at me for a moment through the blue-gray entanglement of his eyebrows. I could see no indication of the terror that usually appeared in a citizen's eyes, but there was nothing to make me think his answer would be different.

Then into our little pool of silence, however, he tossed these shocking words: "That's a good idea, my boy. I will."

This surprised me, of course.—But I felt there was nothing to be dismayed about,—not with the wind blowing across Dewey's desk the way it did. Sometimes we couldn't hold on to all the letters, so bitter and relentless blew the wind. Sometimes it almost whipped a letter out of Dewey's fingers while he was trying to read it.

3

I kept my eyes open for the letter. It did not come in the next day. There was a five-page argument for a literal interpretation of the Bible and two pages of denunciation of the boll-weevil who the writer said, wasn't satisfied with eating up all the cotton but was now sitting on the mailbox waiting to get his teeth in the parity check.—But there was nothing from Cousin Willy.

There was also nothing the next day. It didn't seem like him to have overlooked it; I was amazed when he said he would write, but having said it, he certainly seemed to me like the man to follow it through. I reckoned it would come in in due time; I saw his column there on the hook and I supposed he had been too busy with that to write the letter.

That afternoon, when we had put the last edition on the street, I went downstairs to drink a dope. When I came back the phone on Dewey's desk was ringing like crazy. "*Leader?*" I said.

"Where's Dewey?"

"Dewey stepped out for a minute, Mr. Hoats. Any message?"

The only reply was a bang of the receiver that left me staring off blankly at Rucker and his broom.

In a minute I hung up too. I put a piece of copy paper in Dewey's typewriter, wrote on it, "Mr. H. called—3:54," and left it in the machine. Then on second thought, I backed up and put a couple of exclamation points after the "4."

I turned to the few envelopes of the late mail on Dewey's desk and ran through them for something resembling a letter from Cousin Willy. But there was still no letter. I couldn't figure it.

I was just about to forget it all and go home, when Dewey came in. "Mr. Hoats been trying—"

"I know, I know!"

"You talk to him?"

Dewey shook his head.

"What's going on?" I said.

"Didn't you see it?"

"See what?"

"I didn't read the damn hash, you know. I just put it on the hook. I thought the old guy was writing a war column—"

I snatched a paper and flung it open. There it was: *On the Firing Line,* with a subtitle, "What's all this I hear?"

It was in two parts, with an introduction. The introduction described how there was a movement afoot to change the name of the square from one commemorating the Confederate dead, to one commemorating "a certain Mr. Toolen, one-time resident of this community."

Part One took up Mr. Toolen. I don't know where Cousin Willy got his information, but it was pretty accurate. He conducted Mr. Toolen through six years of grammar school and through the two or three years of his early life in one of the cotton mills, where he became interested in politics through association with local office seekers, whose attitude toward the mill sections was that of a hunter toward a baited field. It

77

was not long before he was lending his abilities to the Streets & Drains Department, and not long thereafter that he conceived the ideal which was to dominate the whole of his lengthy career in the public trust: to eliminate the needless waste of having two or more political parties in Fredericksville, competing and fighting with one another, creating discord and unrest, when all this squandered time and energy could be concentrated in one great brotherhood known as the Home Folks Party, of which he himself would be the patriarchal head.

Then in Part Two Cousin Willy turned to the contribution of the "Confederate dead" to the community, concentrating particularly on the men whose figures adorned the monument,—General Cobb, who "hour after hour held his position in front of Lee's batteries below the Rappahannock, while division after division of the enemy was hurled against him, until at last he was shot through the head and killed;" General Walker, "blocking Sherman's advance into our state at Tanner's Ferry;" ending with an account of Wheeler's cavalry "swimming the Oconee River under the noses of the Union columns" and at Brier Creek, "with a handful of Confederates as nameless now as the figure of that basic rifleman standing at ease on the top of our memorial shaft, turned back Kilpatrick's wing of the invaders as it headed for the great powder mill at Fredericksville."

By the time he got to the bottom of the page, Mr. Toolen looked like a Yankee straggler after the First Battle of Manassas. "Fellow Citizens," Cousin Willy concluded, with a wiggle of his eyebrows, as I read on, half paralyzed, "blood and toil is the price our fathers paid for this Fredericksville of 1940. Are we now, with their deeds ringing in our ears, to sit idly by while—"

I skipped the few remaining lines, having absorbed all I could, and also because the terrible impact of what he had done seemed only now to dawn on me. The fact that he had no doubt done it in all innocence, having been out of civilized life too long to understand the gravity of such an act, didn't make it any the easier for the rest of us. It wasn't so much that it came now at exactly the wrong moment, just as peace and friendship and mutual understanding were taking place between us and Mr. Doc Buden; it would have been just about as bad at any other time. First to come out in the public press with a signed article twice a week, and now to hurl one of them, like a custard pie, at the established government,—well, it was almost beyond words.

Nobody had complained about the government, even in an anonymous letter, for as long as I could remember. Occasionally the *Leader* used to have a mild editorial perhaps advocating this and that, but no private citizen took any such stand. And even if it had taken place on some occasion I couldn't remember, I am sure the letter was not signed and I am sure it did not run a column in length and I am sure it wasn't written by anyone you ever heard of.—That was just not the way we did things in Fredericksville. If you didn't amount to much in the town and wanted something done, like chopping down a tree on the sidewalk or filling up the washes in the street in front of your house or something like that, you just waited and kept your eyes open until you ran into Mr. Doc Buden in front of Bo Peep's Smokehouse and said, "By the way, Doc, look here, I've got a little favor I wish you would do for me," and the Doc would write it down in his book and it would be done on the minute the first thing the next morning; and if you were more or less somebody, you called up your lawyer and he talked to the City Attorney, who spoke to the Streets &

Drains.—To come out on the editorial page—well—

And not the least of it all was my two-fifty a week and the possibility that Mr. Hoats might feel that the chances of its being overlooked by our average subscriber had been greatly diminished by the reader-confidence I had stirred up with my shot of the colonel and his faithful canine—

I folded the paper and gently laid it on a corner of Dewey's desk. I felt a good deal of sympathy for Mr. Hoats; what explanation he was going to offer at the Municipal Building I couldn't see. He might fire Cousin Willy and repudiate the stand in an editorial, but that might be bad too—

I heard Dewey talking over the phone, though I hadn't heard it ring. I thought he might be talking to Mr. Hoats and I listened.

"As far as I can determine, ma'am," Dewey was saying, "it's an unfounded rumor. . . . Thank you, ma'am. We'll certainly do everything we can. . . . The colonel's not in the office at the moment. Mr. Hoats is the editor; he's the man you want to talk to. He'll appreciate your support. . . . Just a minute, I'll connect you."

Dewey turned to the mail, slitting it open, it seemed to me, as if he thought it was Cousin Willy's neck; he went about it all, too, as a man returns to his business routine in the wake of some personal tragedy. Still I thought the call had put a glimmer in his eyes, just a glimmer, of a hope I had not seen there before.

"United Daughters of the Confederacy," he flung out without looking at me. And after a few more envelopes, "Congratulating us!" with a bitter laugh.

I couldn't think of any comforting words.

"You know this old guy," he went on as if determined to make me say something, leaning back in his chair and examining me. "What do you make of him? Is he just a nut, or is he—is he just a nut?"

"I think he just doesn't understand, Dewey."

"You don't reckon this is the string, do you? You don't reckon he offered us this stuff as a war commentary, planning all along to throw something like this at us the first chance he got—"

"No," I insisted. "He's just spent all his life in the army and doesn't understand the world. He'll catch on; just give him a chance."

"What are you and I going to use for money while he's catching on?"

Behind me I heard the well-known squeak of the door hinges. I didn't turn round; I just glanced at

Dewey. Dewey glanced at the door and I could tell by his face who it was.

Mr. Hoats came in with a curious slow saunter. He didn't reply to our simultaneous greeting, but walked round Dewey's desk with his lengthy stride and sat down sideways in a chair. He even glanced at his fingernails.

"How'd it get by you, Dewey?" he said, almost sweetly.

It was a mighty question. I looked round on the desk for a pencil or a ruler I could play with.

Then at that moment, the telephone rang, and Dewey and I nearly ran each other down getting at it; his "Hello" was about a tenth of a second ahead of mine.

"You, Mr. Hoats," Dewey said warmly, putting the receiver with a placating gentleness in Mr. Hoats's hand. We turned away as if having no further interest in the conversation; but when Mr. Hoats said, "Hello, Mr. Manadue," I could almost hear Dewey's ears sitting up.

"Thank you, Mr. Manadue, I appreciate your support. . . . I don't think there's a thing to it. Frankly, Colonel Effingham just went off half cocked, as well

83

as I can make out. . . . Glad you like it, Mr. Mana-due; I figured it was going to make us a nice little feature. . . . Oh, no. Of course not." (I guessed that was where Manadue said not to quote him.)

When Mr. Hoats hung up, he didn't slap the instrument down and swing back to the subject in hand; he laid it down with a certain thoughtfulness and sat there for a minute, silent, looking at it.

"Did the U.D.C. get you, Mr. Hoats?" Dewey inquired solicitously, with a certain constructive wiliness.

Mr. Hoats replied only by laying on Dewey an oblique eye and asking him in a half-mumbled aside if he had heard anything from "round there,"—by which we sometimes referred to the Municipal Building.

"They wouldn't see it unless it was on the Sports Page."

"Somebody'll show it to them."

"It seems to me, Mr. Hoats," Dewey said, no doubt thinking he saw a chance of justifying his not having stopped it, "this thing is signed by a special writer, it doesn't represent the policy of the paper—"

Mr. Hoats interrupted him by getting pensively to his feet, taking a turn to the door of the composing

84

room and back, and then, before our unbelieving eyes, without a word, leaving us.

It seemed like as miraculous a turn of the tide as Kilpatrick being thrown back at Brier Creek. Dewey glanced at me, drew his crooked finger across his forehead and flipped the imaginary cold sweat off on the floor. I didn't know how to interpret it; the Mr. Hoats who went out of the door was certainly not the Mr. Hoats who had set the telephone wires quivering with his "Where's Dewey?"

I didn't know whether he felt that it was too late now to do much about Cousin Willy's piece and that he must throw himself on that tried and trusted expedient of "letting it blow over," or whether, possibly, Mr. Manadue's words had fallen so sweetly on his ears as to undermine his sense of reality.

I guessed it was, on the whole, more of the first. Though he was not a Southerner, he had been round Fredericksville long enough to know that the blow-it-over breeze was in these parts the prevailing current of air and as much to be counted on as a southwest wind in July. It had blown over much more difficult issues than this; the technique, as in any other bombing raid, was to drop prone on the ground and lie still. When, once in the old days, the rumor began to circulate that the equipment in the new water plant was some $50,000 cheaper than the appropriation paid for, everybody hit the ground as one man and didn't move for a month; at length somebody lifted up his head, looked round, listened, and gave the all-clear,—and sure enough it was all clear.

. . . . The next morning on my way to the Municipal Building I couldn't help being impersonal enough to observe that my heels seemed to be dragging a little.

But there was no need for apprehension; nobody mentioned the piece. (The mayor, who had come to us at an early age from South Georgia, later described it as "like finding a rattlesnake in your bureau drawer," but there was no comment that morning.) I didn't know whether they hadn't seen it, or whether their long-nurtured contempt for the written word was standing them in good stead, or whether they were simply prone. Perhaps, also, I didn't hang round there quite as long as usual, though it seemed like a long time.

Anyway, when I left I was breathing considerably easier. That cleansing breeze had already begun to blow and I thought if Mr. Hoats would explain the delicacy of the situation to Cousin Willy with the right emphasis his attitude might turn out to have been merely a sporadic outburst and not, as I realized now I had feared, something chronic.

When I came within sight of the *Leader* building, I saw Cousin Willy's unmistakable figure coming out. I guessed that Mr. Hoats had lost no time in going into the matter; Cousin Willy's stride didn't look as if he had been raked over the coals, though I knew an Effingham would not have paraded his burns if he had them.

"Enjoying the column," I said professionally, as we paused in the shade of a disgusted tree.

"I've just been talking to What's-his-name in there."

I glanced at him again for wounds but I still didn't see any. "How does he feel about it?" I said, all innocence.

"Oh, he seems to like it very much," said Cousin Willy with some satisfaction, as if a little surprised at my question.

"Well," I said, "that's fine, that's fine." I nodded my head to disguise my incredulity.

"He seems to think people here are more interested in the foreign situation than in local matters. He thought perhaps if I confined my comments to the war I might have more readers."

"I see." I started to tell him if he didn't confine his

87

comments to the war he wouldn't have even a proof reader.

"But, floods, boy!" cried Cousin Willy. "Are you proposing to fight dictatorships abroad and submit to one in your home town?"

I felt my head shaking slightly, not so much in negation as in a sort of sadness at the resurgence of what I had thought was diminishing. "You ought to tell that to him, not to me—"

"Oh, I did!"

"Oh, you did?"

"There's no denying that, Albert.—He doesn't think I am close enough yet to the local situation to understand it. But you don't have to be close. An American can smell tyranny a long way off."

"He didn't put any restrictions on you?"

"Restrictions?"

"Well, I thought—"

"You don't have to understand the local situation to recognize an assault on a strategic position."

"But, Colonel, no assault has been made on anybody—"

"Reconnaissance brought to my hand, Albert, information believed to be reliable that an attack was in the final stages of preparation. It was my duty to strike

88

at the concentration, not simply to wait and repel the charge."

I didn't know what to make of this kind of talk. I half expected Cousin Willy to break into a smile, even if it was a grim one. But there was no smile. In fact, I think this was the point at which a more serious and far-reaching apprehension entered my mind: could it be possible that Cousin Willy was deficient in humor?

This uncomfortable thought, of course, served to make our future only darker. Most of us in the South, you know, have a very prominent sense of humor; it works as a stabilizer against excesses, supplementing the action of the climate in discouraging us from acting either too quickly or too positively and so laying ourselves open to a sort of social sunstroke. If we get the idea that something we are about to do may seem funny to somebody, the chances are we won't do it. If it should be true that Cousin Willy's humor was defective, it opened up the most appalling possibilities; it was like coming over the five-thousand foot pass in the Great Smokies and finding your brakes had gone bad.

However, it was at that time just a bleak suspicion in my mind, hardly even put into words.

CHAPTER IV

Now you mustn't get the idea from all this that we put more importance on Cousin Willy's column than we did. It possessed a certain attractiveness for us, being a handout and being written locally and all that, but it was a very small part of the paper and we had other things to think about. I had shown Cousin Willy how to mark his copy for the printer and when it came in it was ready for the hook, all pasted up in a four-foot strip, paragraphs all looped, everything in order down to the little crow's foot at the bottom; he seemed to take to these hieroglyphics as naturally as if they were a military code. One incompleted column he marked "more to kum," which I felt entitled him to his fraternity pin.—What I am getting at is that, except for curiosity (which we hadn't much time for) and a need for censorship, there was no necessity for anybody to read the colonel's copy at all.

After a few days of the blessed breeze, the censor-

ship relaxed again and things began to get back to normal. Dewey revised his editorial slightly to fit the new
circumstances, as you might detour round an unex-
pected bomb crater, and had it set up. It was now to
be offered in the spirit of righting a wrong. A certain
one of our independent columnists, over whom we took
pride in exercising no control and to whom we granted
full privilege of expressing his opinions ("we may not
agree with what he says," we cried, "but we will defend to the death his right to say it"), we felt had not
done justice to that genial old character, that kindly
old citizen and civic leader to whom no friend was too
small and none too great, that noblest Roman of them
all, Pud Toolen. The touches about the Roman and
the right to speak were added by Mr. Hoats with his
thick pencil,—necessitating the resetting of six inches
of type, though of course it was worth it.

We set it in the forms for our Sunday edition, which
we published in the morning, and I read it over my
sausage and hominy in the Manhattan Café while little
groups of hypothetical voters in tighter shoes than
usual hurried along past the closed stores toward the
high bells ringing somewhere behind my left shoulder.
I saw Mr. Doc Buden go by, with a little of that same
self-consciousness at being publicly surrounded by

his women-folk as a young husband in pushing a new baby carriage; I thought he glanced at the window which framed me and my hominy like a surrealist painting, but as I nodded he looked away and I reckoned he hadn't seen me on account of the reflections in the glass.

By the time I started on my second cup of coffee (which Sadie brought me unbidden every Sunday morning, setting it down on the paved table with a motherly solicitude that sent a sort of jerk through my neural network for its subtle counterpoint of sacred and profane love), and lighted my weekly indulgence of a five-cent cigar, the church bells had stopped ringing and the streets looked like an illuminated three A. M. I glanced at the other editorials and then, as if by chance, so completely had I forgotten Cousin Willy in the pleasant glow of Dewey's full-measured retribution, my eye fell on the 36-point Bodoni of "*On the Firing Line.*" I settled back, full of hominy and coffee and good will, settled back with a benignant smile for Cousin Willy and all my kin,—settled back to catch up on the war.

"On another occasion," began Cousin Willy, "I have pointed out the relative value for purposes of memorial of a certain Mr. Toolen and our Confederate dead—"

Everything faded out a little for me; the cigar began

to taste as if it were getting ready to burn up one side.

"A community's history is its family tree," said Cousin Willy. "You and I are descendants of our fathers, but Fredericksville is the descendant of the Battle of Kettle Creek where Elijah Clarke broke the British hold on upper Georgia, of the Battle of the Sand Bar Ferry which saved Fredericksville a second time from Sherman's torch, of Jeb Stuart's cavalry and General Lee's barefoot columns. The spiritual soil of Fredericksville is rich today because yesterday its Citizens ploughed into it their toil and their blood. Fredericksville did not spring like a mushroom over-night out of the molded earth; it was wrested by steady hand and steady eye from the reluctant wilderness, wrested from the British King's tyranny, wrested from Sherman, wrested from the noxious mire of defeat and reparations.—Can it be that this seventh generation of warriors is so faint of heart as to surrender intact this fortress we have built to the birds of prey—"

"Anything the matter with the coffee, Al?"

I shook my head absentmindedly, the cigar tasting worse and worse, the hominy getting heavier and heavier on my chest.

"This plan to change the name of our honored square

93

is a trifling with our sturdy history. We shall not submit to it; the Sons of Liberty once gathered in the Long Room of Tondee's Tavern and we shall find gathering places for them today. Yet it is not enough that we stand to the defense and hold the name of the square as it has been for near a century; let us move through the sally ports to the field. Let us improve the square as a memorial to the Lost Cause. Picture, if you will, in a circle about that shaft of Georgia marble, thirteen live-oak trees, one for each member of that glorious alliance—"

Sadie brought me a hot cup of coffee. "Everything all right, Al?"

"Have you seen this?" I said.

She leaned over the table and looked at the column. "He wants to plant trees round the monument," I explained. "Thirteen trees—"

"I read that," she said. "That would be nice; nice shade. It's nice to see leaves blowing in the summertime—"

I couldn't help slapping my forehead. "But every year or two somebody brings up trees—"

"Well, Gee! Where would we be without trees?"

"Do you want this place to look like a country town? —And anyhow they're not going to do it and what's

94

the use in bringing it all up again and trying to embarrass everybody—"

"Well, Gee! I never heard of a tree embarrassing anybody—"

"Everything going right, Al?" said Jimmy, the boss, leaving his cigar counter and shooing Sadie away with his folded paper. Jimmy was a Greek whose name had been reforged under the heat of our democracy into James Economy; he was also the man who told the down-and-outer who ate the Manhattan's Number 5 Dinner and then couldn't pay for it, "All right, but just don't give me all your business."

I turned away and looked at the window and the back side of that curious shape which, seen from the sidewalk, was recognizable to the imaginative as a beaver hat in consideration of the second syllable of Manhattan. That hat was Jimmy's pride and whenever I happened to see it after a couple of drinks on Saturday night, I was likely to become philosophical in my best undergraduate manner and argue that in ordering that hat for his sign you had proof that Mr. Economy was an artist; there was no art in the hat, but, in the fact that Jimmy had wanted a sign that was a little bit more than merely explanatory, you saw the seed of the art instinct, from the Parthenon down.

"Tell me, Jimmy," I said, when he had whipped a chair up to the end of my table and seated himself voluminously upon it. "Do you ever see this little piece we run sometimes called '*On the Firing Line*'?"

"Yeah, yeah, sure."

"You do? Well, tell me, Jimmy, what do you make of it?"

"I think that guy's got something; some nice trees out there round the monument—"

"But, Jimmy—"

"A little something spent for beauty, Al, is a good buy."

"But, Jimmy, the trees wouldn't grow, for one thing, and they cost money, for another, and for another—tell me, Jimmy, did you read what this column said the other day about changing the name of the square?"

"Oh, yeah, sure. We always read it. Seems like a nice sort of fellow,—nice dog he had in that picture."

I said, "Um-humh," or something like that.

"My wife cut out that picture. Lots of people like that picture. Who took—"

"I want to use your telephone, Jimmy."

"Sure, help yourself."

I thought I ought to run out and talk to Cousin Willy; things were going too far. It was almost rude;

it was almost like getting up in church and nagging the preacher. Of course Cousin Willy just didn't understand, but that didn't affect the rudeness of it. It seemed to me something the family ought to explain to him. Something, as a matter of fact, that Cousin Emma might could do better than I—

The cook answered and I asked for Miss Emma.

"Miss Emma gone to church," the cook said in the tone you might expect if you called somebody at two A. M. and was told he had gone to bed.

I didn't know which church she belonged to, but she was a Marbury and our family would as soon have been caught going to Mass as to any but the First Methodist. I got my hat and walked round there.

I stood out on the curb in front of the church, feeling pretty unwashed and grimy, until the organ pealed its dismissal and the beige doors all across the front were simultaneously opened by Commissioner Loren Mitts, a junior vice-president of the Farmers Bank & Trust named Topp, and the mayor's secretary, Mr. Box Smith, —all of them looking very much relaxed, as when a fire has been put out. Among the first to emerge were the county clerk and Mr. Eurus, the tax receiver (who passed the plate, amid a good many friendly quips about taxes) and who occupied the pews in the rear.

After a while I saw Cousin Emma, a small, bright-eyed woman in dark blue; I waited until she had finished her after-church conversation with some friends and begun to look about for Ninety-eight.

"Cousin Emma," I said.

"Why, Albert, you've been to church?"

"Could I see you for a minute, Cousin Emma?"

She invited me into the back seat of the colonel's Ford; I told Ninety-eight we were not ready to go yet: "You wait out here. I'll call you." Then I crawled in.

"Cousin Emma," I said, not knowing just how to begin, but determined. "Well, you've been reading the column, I reckon."

"Of course I have—"

"You read it this morning?"

"Oh, yes. And you know the Ladies' Memorial Association, Clara Meigs is president, they think it's a wonderful idea. And not only that, but Will has talked to the nursery and dear Mr. Dobey is going to give the trees. Give them, you hear!—Will says the only thing we need now are some holes and two loads of stable manure—"

"Yes'm, but—"

"Will said he could take Ninety-eight down there with a good shovel and dig the holes in half a day."

I blanched, even though it was a joke, and Cousin Emma laughed in a pleasant tinkle, adding, "Will's a sight!"

I was certainly in no mood to deny that Will was a sight; but I did think there might be some possibility that Cousin Emma could suggest something to do about it.

"But the thing is, Cousin Emma, this is not the way to go at it. The colonel is a responsible citizen here; he is in a position to have some influence—"

"That's just it, Albert."

"But men in responsible positions just don't write about local matters in the newspapers."

"Why, I think it's grand for some nice person to take an interest in the monument."

"Cousin Emma," I said, "it's all right to take an interest in the monument, but there is a way to do it. If you want trees round the monument the thing to do is go talk to Mr. Doc Buden—"

"I never heard of any such person."

"He has the barbershop concession at the hotel," I explained, "and you really should have heard of him."

"Can you imagine Will talking to—"

"Listen, Cousin Emma. If you want to have turnip greens for dinner, what do you do? Do you call in the cook and have a talk about it,—or do you go out on the front porch and start telling everybody in the street you want turnip greens?"

"Albert!"

"The point is that twice now within a month a responsible citizen, the very kind of person you would least expect to do such a thing, has come out in what amounts to an open attack on the government. I know he didn't do it with any malice—"

"Do you think it's that serious, Albert?"

"When an Effingham proposed writing a war commentary under his own name,—well, though nothing like that had ever happened in Fredericksville before, it seemed in a worthy cause, and after all this is 1940. But now to suddenly swing about in two unprovoked attacks on our civic leaders,—why, it's almost an outright double cross.—And aside from that, the position he puts the paper in is very painful. Mr. Hoats overlooked it the first time, but now I frankly don't see what he can do but stop the column."

"Will would write it for the *News;* he doesn't care."

"They wouldn't touch it," I said, hoping I knew what I was talking about.

"What's so awful about putting a few trees round the monument?"

"It's the way he went at it. It's just—well, Cousin Emma, I hate to say it, but it's just tacky."

"You know, Albert," Cousin Emma said with a smile, getting ready to deal me one of the worst blows I had had since the moment I began to suspect Cousin Willy might not be adequately equipped with humor, "he said to me the other day, he said, 'Emma, it's such a pleasure to be getting old, because you can say so many things you've always felt but for one reason or another were scared to say before—'"

I felt my breath go out of me almost as if I had been punched in the stomach.

"He said when you get to be upwards of sixty there's no use in saving your grudges much longer."

"You mean he's going to use this column—" I ran out of words and Cousin Emma chirped in pleasantly.

"Goodness, Albert, I don't know what he's going to do. You come out and talk to him—"

I backed out of the car and signalled Ninety-eight with a speechless finger.

2

The repercussions were what you might have expected. Bright and early Monday morning Mr. Hoats called Dewey into his office, let go with a good deal of

understandable indignation about how the *Leader* was
not going to be a party to any such subversive activi-
ties against the government, and told Dewey to fire
Colonel Effingham.

"Don't you think you ought to do it?" said Dewey,
naturally not taking to the job much. "You hired him."

"Don't argue with me. Fire him."

Dewey came over to the newsroom pretty disconso-
late,—not, of course, at the prospect of Cousin Willy
without a job but at the prospect of breaking the news
to him. We didn't know Cousin Willy very well; all
we knew was, so to speak, what we had read in the paper, and from that it looked as if Cousin Willy had
more words than we had. I don't know why a little
thing like that should make any difference, but it seemed
to. It reminded me of my school days and the question
that used to bother me of why one teacher could keep
discipline and another couldn't. The ultimate punish-
ment was in all cases the same, but one man could do
it and another couldn't; I used to think it was words
that made the difference, that we dreaded more being
lashed by a few well-chosen phrases than by the rod.

"I hate to fire the old guy," Dewey said, his heart
bleeding for him.

"I'd hate to myself," I said. But I also couldn't help

being sorry to see a member of the family getting the sack. "It looks to me like we'd just be handing him to the *News* on a silver platter—"

"What's the matter with him? Does he want a job with the city? Are his taxes too high?—What's he mad about?"

I shook my head. I had my own ideas on it, but they were largely guesswork and, out of mere family loyalty, I didn't like to mention anything so indefinite as that it seemed to me, if we weren't careful we might find ourselves confronted by integrity on the rampage. "I figure he's just green, Dewey. He'd be a good man for us if he could understand the setup."

"You think there's any use talking to him?"

I didn't answer for a minute because I thought I was beginning to see a new angle on it. "Look here, Dewey. Suppose he doesn't see it eye to eye with us. Maybe it's better if he doesn't. There are some people round here who may see it his way, not many but some. Get him to tone it down a little bit, that's all we need. He can't hurt the Home Folks; let him say anything he wants to outside of downright libel. That gives us, don't you see, a nice toehold on both sides of the fence—"

"Let's go talk to Earl."

Mr. Hoats was still mad. But he looked at his cigar

ash for a full ten seconds when we explained how the colonel might work out to keep the paper in touch with a certain element that might be tempted to lose faith in us if we let him go; he didn't seem to put any stock in my fear that the *News* might take him on,—but the outcome was that I should talk to him, calm him down a little, see what the trouble was.

"We don't mind playing ball," Mr. Hoats said; "we just don't know what kind of ball this is he's trying to play.—And you might explain to him, on the other hand, that the Board of Assessors meets now and then and he may find his house worth a lot more than he ever would have dreamed possible."

"Let me just see what he says, Mr. Hoats. He's nobody's fool."

"Well, we can all have our own opinions about that."

"Let me talk to him—"

"Talk to him, then! All I know is that this sort of thing of trying to undermine the government won't be tolerated in the *Leader*. Why, that's what the war's all about, trying to preserve the American form of government—"

I think we all felt better about it. I know Dewey did.

I hopped a bus and went out to see him.

. . . . I found Cousin Willy sitting on the old south-

104

west escarpment. Ninety-eight was leaning a shoulder against one of the cedar trees, occasionally glancing up at a limb that was just too high to afford him any prehensile support, and watching the end of the colonel's walking stick as it surveyed the line of the river and the old creek flowing into it between Fort Frederick and the outpost at Fort Grierson.

"But were the Patriots satisfied to leave Fredericksville in the hands of the enemy?" Cousin Willy was saying.

The question being way out of sight, Ninety-eight shook his head.

"Precisely," said Cousin Willy, jabbing the stick into the sand. "And one day—sit down, Albert,—one day they came back, sorry to pay the price, of course, but determined to have Fredericksville."

I heaved a quiet sigh and joined Major Jackson's Rangers in the canebrake along the branch. The rising sun was drawing the steam out of the cane; there was a slight wind in the tops of the pines but it didn't get down to us, and the mosquitoes whined peacefully about our faces. I didn't like it; I knew there were snakes in there as long as my rifle and bigger around.

But when Clarke opened up on Grierson from our left, and Lee, across the creek in a mulberry grove on our right, opened up on Brown in Fort Frederick to prevent his sending reinforcements to Grierson, things began to get so animated we forgot the mosquitoes and the snakes too. We ploughed on down the lagoon, up to our knees in muck, the smell of powder smoke drifting into the swamp.

Then, as we came opposite the east gate, Grierson threw it open and made a dash for it; the whole garrison came scuttling out of there like rats and headed pell-mell across the open field for the river bank. We were after them with a yelp, pouring a deadly fire into their flank.

Hardly a man reached Fort Frederick. Two of the Rangers brought in Colonel Grierson himself, both leggings gone, his shirt torn half off his back. "Sit down, Colonel," said Cousin Willy, stern but magnanimous too.

We didn't get to cross-question Grierson because the balance of thrusts which had kept Ninety-eight's body securely propped against the cedar somehow seemed to get out of kilter; it began to slip, and he gained consciousness only just in time to keep from rolling down the terreplein into a traverse.

Cousin Willy sent him to the rear like any other walking casualty.

But the incident had brought us up to date and in a few minutes Cousin Willy said, "I'm glad you came out, Albert. I've been wanting to talk to you about this memorial to the Confederacy."

It was a great relief to have the mention of it come from him. I hadn't known just how I was going to bring it up; now that I was face to face with him, it seemed so much more personal than it had at the office.

"I thought you might know better than I just what would be the attitude of the local government about these trees—"

I told him I thought I might be able to give a rough guess.

"I suppose I ought to give them some indication of what we are going to do."

"Colonel," I began.

"You see, the Ladies' Memorial Association has invited me to make them a little talk about planting the trees round the monument. Well, that's all right. But I believe in action. Let's plant the trees and then talk about it.—Now what I should like to know is do you think the city government could have any possible objection to our planting the trees?"

"Well, it's a little irregular—"

"What's irregular about it?"

"It's about as irregular," I said, "as trying to squeeze juice back into an orange."

"There's no question of squeezing," said Cousin Willy; "we're giving them the trees.—What I thought I should do would be to take Ninety-eight down there tomorrow with his shovel and get the holes lined up—"

"Colonel—"

"Dobey has given us the trees and—"

"Colonel—"

"I don't want him to have to dig the holes after he has been generous enough—"

"Colonel," I insisted, "you know the mayor, don't you?"

Cousin Willy said he had not the pleasure of knowing His Honor. I couldn't tell whether the expression was ironic or simply old-fashioned, but I let it go. "The mayor is a garden-fancier. He loves trees and flowers. He's got all the equipment for setting out trees—"

"You don't need any equipment."

"It might be, if he was interested, you could set out bigger trees. Anyway, it seems to me it would be nice to consult him; he would naturally like to be in on some civic improvement like this, like a little of the credit."

"I don't care anything about the credit; I want the trees."

"Exactly; let them have the credit. You see,—you see, they were going to change the name of the square, then people started talking about it and now they've got to lie flat for a few weeks until things quiet down. They might welcome the chance of the trees just to show their heart's in the right place."

"I don't know, Albert, whether their heart's in the right place or not."

"Oh, they're nice fellows. You just don't know them well yet. They want to do what's right. You mustn't forget, Colonel, they haven't had all the advantages of education and travel and that sort of thing some of the rest of us have had. You'd be surprised at where some of them have come from—"

"It wouldn't surprise me at all," said Cousin Willy, "but I don't see why the biggest and most important project in Habersham County, the administration of the government, should be handed, lock, stock, and barrel, to the underprivileged."

I laughed with as much deprecation of his words as I could, but I dare say it had a strange ring because I began to wonder seriously now if maybe Cousin Willy was really in earnest. I had thought he was interested

primarily in the war, and had thrown in these few columns about other things for a little variety; I hadn't
considered he might really go into the situation.

"Colonel," I said, "I don't think you are quite giving
the boys their due—"

"Due!" said Cousin Willy. "When we turned on the
malarial mosquitoes in the Canal Zone, do you think
they were not getting their due?"

"That's not quite the way it is, sir."

"Fredericksville's future lies blocked in a jungle of
petty intrigue," said Cousin Willy, getting that look in
his eye, "blocked in murky swamps, preyed upon by
great pestilential swarms of politicians bearing malaria,
yellow fever, all manner of communal diseases, sapping
the strength of the Citizens, preventing them from shap-
ing Fredericksville's true destiny, from digging Fredericksville's true course through the years. As on the
Isthmus, these noxious elements must be dealt with before anything else can be accomplished—"

"But, Colonel," I said, "somebody has got to run the
government of Fredericksville. The citizens won't do
it; if it wasn't for the Home Folks there wouldn't be
any government at all."

"Is it your impression, Albert, that these people are
acting more or less as trustees until such time as the

Citizens come of age and can take over the government themselves?"

That was more than I could answer; I was already over my head. "Anyhow," I said, "I think you ought to have a chat with the mayor sometime—"

"All right, Albert, I will."

"Good." I thought at least I could go back to the office and report a slight improvement, a slight possibility that the crisis was going to be postponed.

He stood up. "Can I drop you by your office?"

"You going into town anyway? I can pick up a bus—"

"I'm going to the Municipal Building."

"You going to see the mayor now?"

"Certainly, Albert."

"There's no hurry, Cousin Willy!" I almost squealed. "Any old time—"

"Son," he said, giving me a light-hearted pat on the shoulder and speaking as off-handedly as if talking about catching a train later in the day, "when you get to be sixty-five, it's a good time to hurry."

3

Cousin Willy devoted two or three wide-eyed columns to his wanderings in Municipalia, describing the

flora and fauna with something between the sunny innocence of Herodotus or Bartram and the more precise
detail of the Commentaries on the Invasion of Gaul.
Both Dewey and I read the copy (I with mere curiosity
but Dewey with the understandable determination that
he was not going to be caught again), and we decided
there was nothing in them anybody could possibly ob-
ject to,—simple, straight-out accounts such as you or I
might write of a trip down into a coal mine. It is true
that the effect of them was somehow cumulative and
there might have been eventually a few skeptical citizens who began to wonder if their communal destinies
were being guided by all the alert, progressive means
available in this day of science and education. This
would have been misleading, of course; the trouble, in
a word, was simply that nobody knew where to put his
hand on any machinery for handling an incoming concession; to concede something to the city caused about
as much consternation as to try to swing your truck
eastward into a west-bound street.—But to all appear-
ances, Cousin Willy was just describing his travels.

The boys at the Municipal Building were not very
happy about it; they seemed to feel there must be more
to the articles than met the eye, but they have always

been skittish about the press anyhow. And then too, they couldn't overlook the fact, which apparently everybody else had overlooked, that the more talk there was about planting these trees to the Confederacy, the farther they were getting away from the original proposition of changing the name of the square.

Cousin Willy had begun his wanderings at the grille inside the door protecting the Sheriff's Office. "Can you direct me to His Honor the Mayor?" he inquired.

Mr. Thurtig looked up from a ledger as big as a doormat and with corners considerably worse used; he studied Cousin Willy quizzically for a second, naturally not being altogether satisfied about that "his honor."

"End of the hall," he said, pointing with his wooden pen. Cousin Willy saluted him with the handle of his stick to his helmet brim.

He paused in an open door, beyond which Mr. Box Smith in his shirtsleeves was reading a paper with his feet on the golden-oak double desk. "Would it be possible for me to see His Honor the Mayor?" said Cousin Willy.

Mr. Box Smith laid the paper on his knees. "The mayor's in conference; is there anything I can do for you?"

"Well," said Cousin Willy with a smile, putting his helmet under his left arm, "I don't know. Who are you?"

Mr. Smith's feet seemed to fall off the desk. "I'm the mayor's secretary."

"I am Colonel Effingham, Mr. Secretary," said Cousin Willy. "W. Seaborn Effingham, Colonel United States Army, retired. Would you be so good as to ask how long it will be before I can see His Honor?"

Mr. Smith went into the adjoining office and after a few minutes returned to the doorway. "Are you here, Colonel, in connection with National Defense?"

"Oh, yes," said Cousin Willy easily. "Nothing makes any difference now but the defense of America."

The secretary blinked his eyes a couple of times, disappeared again, and in a moment came back to say the mayor would see him now.

Cousin Willy thanked him for his trouble and walked into a big bare office where a man of forty or so, with the jowls that public service seems to develop in its adherents as surely as moving pianos develops the biceps, was signing something at his desk under a ceiling fan. He half rose and extended his hand: "Your name is familiar to me, Colonel, but I can't put my finger on just where I've run into it before."

"There have been Effinghams in Fredericksville for a long time," said Cousin Willy.

"Oh," said the mayor, "you mean the government has sent you back to your old home town?"

"I am retired, Your Honor. Uncle Sam has turned me out to graze."

"But you say you are connected with National Defense?"

"By all means," said Cousin Willy. "The defense of America is the nearest thing to my heart. Nothing else matters to me any more, Mr. Mayor, except the preservation of the republican form of government."

"Republican?" said the mayor skeptically.

"Now what I want to discuss with you, Mr. Mayor," Cousin Willy continued, "is the desirability of certain trees on Broad Street."

"But what's that got to do with National Defense, Colonel?"

Cousin Willy leaned over and tapped gently with his finger tips on the mayor's desk: "The same thing as making sure that your lines of communication and supply are properly defended."

The mayor glanced at Cousin Willy in some dismay, partly because of a metaphor he didn't grasp, partly because of the half-formed suspicion that he had let himself in for something.

"Our communications must be kept open all the way back from the front line of democracy in Europe to the smallest courthouse in the smallest county-seat in the nation. If they are cut at any point by tyranny, we are lost!" He slapped the desk and sat back, while the mayor scrutinized the call-bell button.

"There is no threat against the courthouse," said the mayor, considerably bewildered. "It is just so old and dilapidated it is endangering the lives of the county employees. It was built around eighteen hundred, Colonel."

"Courthouse?" said Cousin Willy, moving his eyebrows up then down.

"You mentioned the courthouse, didn't you?"

Cousin Willy got to his feet and in a minute continued, not being as nimble as formerly in skipping his thread of argument, "What I wish to discuss with you, sir, is the planting of thirteen trees in a circle about the Confederate Monument—"

The mayor interrupted him with a sudden gesture, as if he had found something he had lost: "You write that column in the *Leader!*"

"I do."

116

"I knew your name was familiar to me—"

"That's very kind of you, sir."

The mayor lapsed into a silence deeper than before, as Cousin Willy went on. "Knowing you were something of a horticulturist—"

"Colonel," said the mayor, at last getting hold of himself, "let me save you a lot of time and energy. The city at this moment is carrying a note at the Farmers Bank & Trust for fourteen thousand dollars. It is absolutely out of the question to spend another penny that is not necessary."

"I have nothing but praise for your spirit of economy, sir. That is why it gives me such pleasure to tell you the trees have been donated by a public-spirited nurseryman and will not cost the city one copper."

"Donated?" said the mayor, smelling a rat; every nurseryman he knew was a responsible businessman and no responsible businessman ever donated anything to the city. "It sounds like a clever publicity stunt, Colonel. The city government doesn't take part in anything like that."

"No, Tom Dobey is an old friend of mine—"

"And there's also the cost of transplanting them."

"I am taking care of that myself," said Cousin Willy. The mayor laid his paper cutter down on his desk, satisfied now that he was in the presence of a madman and wondering just how he could get rid of him without making him violent.

"And there's also the upkeep, and the cost of watering them through the summer until they get established—"

"The Ladies' Memorial Association has agreed to take care of that," said Cousin Willy. "The whole thing won't cost the city one farthing."

"You represent the Ladies' Memorial Association?"

"I represent a considerable force of men and women who have written me and telephoned me endorsing the plan. It is true their names are not familiar to me, but they are all Citizens of this community—"

"That's pretty vague—"

"I appreciate, sir," said Cousin Willy, "the necessity in our early days for clearing the trees from the parade about the fort and providing our troops with an unobstructed field of fire, but nowadays, when trade is carried on in a more temperate spirit and the value of concealment not so great, there is no necessity for keeping the parade clear—"

"There's a water main under there that might be disturbed. I tell you what you do, Colonel. You understand there's nobody in Habersham County loves trees more than I do; any sort of beautification appeals to me. But it has got to be practical; you can't dig up a water main just to set out a few trees. You go talk to Mr. Clemmer, the City Engineer. I couldn't do a thing without his approval."

The mayor stood up with a good deal of the surprised pleasure at remembering the City Engineer that a man feels at finding a nickel in the pocket of an old suit. "Glad to have seen you, Colonel. Any time I can be of service—"

Out in the wide hall, Cousin Willy didn't stop to examine the interview in retrospect; he pushed ahead through the tangles of a Panama jungle at the head of his scouts, his eyes and ears open, picking his way. If it was impossible to take their objective by a frontal assault, he would simply lead his forces round and try it from the flank.

When he located the command post of the City Engineer he rapped on the door and entered. After identifying himself, he said to Mr. Clemmer, "I only need to take up a minute of your time, sir—"

"Have a chair," said Mr. Clemmer agreeably.

"All I want to know, sir, is are there water mains running underneath Monument Square?"

The abruptness of this rocked Mr. Clemmer back for

a minute. "Well—er—that is not the kind of information I am at liberty to divulge in times like these—"

Cousin Willy interrupted him to tell him about the trees, about what the mayor had said, about how the project would first have to have the approval of the City Engineer.

"I see, I see," said Mr. Clemmer. "Well, we couldn't buy these trees from you; we have our regular—"

"You don't buy them from anybody," Cousin Willy explained patiently.

"How do I get them, raise them from little seeds?"

"They're a gift," said Cousin Willy.

"I don't understand."

"They're free."

Mr. Clemmer shook his head with a canny smile as if he had surprised some boys in the act of pegging his doorbell on Hallowe'en. He got up, walked to the door of the anteroom and closed it. Then he came back and handed Cousin Willy a cigar, sitting down and leaning on the elbow nearest him. "Tell me where you're trying to go, mister, and maybe I can help you."

"An old friend of mine is endeavoring to donate thirteen trees to the city to be planted round the Confederate Monument. It won't cost you a farthing; all I want to know is whether there is a water main they would interfere with—"

Mr. Clemmer gave it up. "The man you want to see is the City Electrician. There may be all kinds of wires running round under there."

. . . . And so it went.

It was several days before Cousin Willy could find the City Electrician, who was chairman of a BPOE Entertainment Committee and engaged in locating an adequate pig.

From there he was forwarded to the Streets & Drains Department, who told him to go see the chairman of the Parks & Trees Commission.

"Where can I find him?" said Cousin Willy, with no more idea of being discouraged than Sheridan trying to locate Stonewall Jackson in the Valley of Virginia.

"He works in the machine shops of the G & A Railroad, but you can probably catch him at home."

Cousin Willy finally found him and sat down on his porch in a wooden swing, posting Ninety-eight on the curb by the car as a routine security measure. At last, he felt, he had reached headquarters; the chairman of the Parks & Trees sounded like the man he had been looking for all along.

"What I'd suggest that you did, sir," the chairman said slowly, weighing his words, having listened patiently to Cousin Willy's Estimate of the Situation, "would be to go round to the Municipal Building and have a talk with the mayor. He's the man you want to see."

. . . . "Orderly," said Cousin Willy, as they drove away, "you've got a good shovel, haven't you?"

"Needs sharpening a little," said Ninety-eight critically.

"What do you need to sharpen it?"

"Oh, a Number Two file."

"Stop at the first hardware store, orderly, and get yourself a file. Tomorrow morning, first thing, I've got a little job I want you to do."

CHAPTER V

Fortunately for everybody concerned—the Effinghams, the Marburys, indeed, Fredericksville itself—there had been other things afoot while the colonel was on tour and nothing was to come of his exasperation, of his evident intention to halt where he was and, quite literally, to dig in. We were consequently spared a scene at our Confederate Monument between Cousin Willy with his shovel and the cold hand of the law that might have taken its place in the annals of Georgia beside the fracas in colonial Savannah when the Royal Government discovered on the King's birthday that the Sons of Liberty had spiked all the cannon on the bay with which His Majesty was to be saluted and rolled them to the bottom of the bluff.

By Heaven's grace, as Ninety-eight was putting the finishing strokes on the edge of the shovel, Cousin Willy unfolded his afternoon *Leader* and read a headline across the top of Page One that stopped him in his tracks as effectively as a raiding party to the shores of German-occupied France would be stopped by a dispatch announcing the invasion of Britain.

I can't be sure that this move by the authorities was intended to avert the engagement pending at Monument Square; certainly such considerable concentrations could not have been brought up overnight. It is likeliest, I feel, that the attack was planned long before but that this particular moment seemed propitious to launch it both because the talk about trees would divert attention from it and also because it would divert attention from the trees. The colonel later described it as a "reinforcement by diversion."

Anyway, at about the time Cousin Willy was talking to the Streets & Drains, Mr. Hoats was talking to Mr. Country Thigman.

Mr. Country Thigman had the Package Shop concession at one of the more informal hotels. He never touched a drop of "package" himself, indeed he rarely so much as cast his shadow over the shelves of bottles, but the Package Shop was officially headquarters and if you wanted to get in touch with him you could leave your number there and after a while, sure enough, he would call you.

Now as you no doubt know, in the South it is a long

time between breakfast and dinner; the result of this is that along about eleven o'clock you feel as if you had done a day's work and yet the day has hardly warmed up. What you do is get your hat and "step round on Broad Street for a minute."

When Mr. Hoats stepped round to Mr. Bo Peep's Smokehouse at about eleven thirty, Mr. Country Thigman was standing in front of the pie counter with his hands locked behind his solid back. It was "Hey, Country" and "Hey, Earl," and they sauntered together out into the current of air before the newsstand.

Then without any preparation at all, Mr. Thigman, comfortably studying the traffic, without anything resembling a smile, said, "What's all this about planting trees, Earl? You want to make us look like a hick town?"

Mr. Hoats stirred up a laugh that he hoped was going to sound heartfelt but that he knew, as soon as he heard it, did not. "Oh, our new column!"

"You want to make us look like Berzelia?"

"That's not me, Country. I don't run that strip any more than I do Barney Google."

"You ought to check on it, Earl. The merchants round here don't want trees, you know, blocking out their signs, stopping up their gutters. You wouldn't want them to think you didn't have their best interests at heart."

"Nobody takes that column seriously, Country—"

"But you're putting the bug on the party, Earl.—You wouldn't want all these merchants to turn their advertising over to the *News*."

Mr. Hoats gulped, as well an editor might: "It's just a joke, Country."

"They might get the idea it wasn't to their advantage to keep on advertising in a paper always trying to stir up trouble."

"Country, you know we're not trying to stir up—"

"All this talk about trees, Earl, it just makes people unhappy, just creates dissatisfaction. We were getting along all right, everybody contented, everybody going about his own business. Then we thought it would be appropriate to beautify the square as a memorial to Pud, one of the grandest old souls that ever breathed the breath of life,—and you throw your influence in the path of progress and civic—"

"It just got by me, Country—"

"We're not opposed to planting trees; but we're just not going to have some foreigner coming in here telling us what we can do and what we can't, meddling in public affairs."

"I know how you feel, Country."

"Trying to donate things to the city, like we couldn't afford to buy what we need."

"I know."

"But all that's over the dam. We're interested in the future, not the past.—We just hope you're not going to stand in the path of progress on this matter of the new courthouse." He might just as well have quietly lifted a water moccasin out of his pants pocket.

"New courthouse!"

"This old courthouse is not only a disgrace to the city and county but it's actually dangerous. It's falling down."

"I didn't know that."

"You go down, look. We had to rope off the back steps."

"I knew that, but I didn't know the whole thing—"

"The whole thing!—And what do you expect? It's been there over a hundred years."

"Well, well, so you gonna—"

"We got to. We can't have this thing falling down and crushing forty or fifty people—"

"Where can I get the story?" said Mr. Hoats, astir like an old fire horse.

"There's a meeting of the Council tomorrow morning to take up the matter. You might want to stop by yourself—"

. . . . Mr. Hoats took me along to do the dirty work of putting it all into words. We walked down together but it was pretty uncongenial; he didn't say much. I thought there was determination in his jaw, the determination of the sinner who has been unexpectedly (and undeservedly) granted a second opportunity to make good, or as our idiom has it, to "get right." He had already sent our photographer down there to get a shot of the rope across the steps and the sign, "Danger—Use Other Entrance."

We climbed over the rope and joined a group of officials in the broad dim hall, gathered about the newel post of the old oval staircase with the wrought-iron lamp bracket; they were gazing suspiciously at a patch of dark laths in the ceiling about the shape of Australia. They shook hands with Mr. Hoats and nodded to me, gravely; there was in it all something of the atmosphere of a coroner's inquest, as if the hole in the plaster above us were the wound from which the old wreck's life blood had ebbed away. Their general soberness seemed merely decent.

"How long has this thing been here?" said Mr. Hoats, bouncing cooperatively on the old beams.

"Lord only knows."

"No wonder it's falling down." He was obviously very much relieved to be back among the blessed, and I must confess I, too, found his safe arrival up there reassuring in the extreme. I gave the old mahogany banisters a resounding shake to show them where I stood in all this.

They took us on a little tour. "Termites," one of the contractors said, pointing to a hole they had sawed in the basement floor; Mr. Hoats shook his head in sympathy and I did the same. There was also a long crack in the brick wall built to house the boiler of the furnace. An engineer took out his pocket knife and scraped some mortar from between the bricks. "Hold on there!" somebody said. "Let me get out of here before you scratch any more." The engineer laughed but the officials didn't respond by much more than a grim smile.

We went into session in an upstairs room with a sixteen-foot ceiling and a mantelpiece carved with a great sunburst medallion. After some minor business, the chair brought up the matter of the building and had the secretary read the reports of the contractors on the condition of the structure. They sounded like somebody in Berlin describing Democracy: the floor construction was unsafe, the stone was disintegrated, the keystones of the windows were loose. The roof was worn out, the walls were unsound, the plaster was dangerous; the plumbing was unsanitary, the heating inadequate, the ventilation unsuitable, the electrical work a fire hazard—

"May I have a copy of that," I said, when he finished, wanting it for my story and, frankly, wanting Mr. Hoats to see I was on my toes.

The chair handed me a copy with one hand, turning to one of the contractors and putting him on the grill to show everything was regular: "Mr. Sink, you are a local contractor, are you not?"

"I am," said Mr. Sink.

"And you have heard the description of the condition of this building?"

"I have."

"Do you concur in these findings you have heard?"

"I do."

"Now, Mr. Sink, will you just tell these gentlemen in your own words why you think it would be unwise to attempt to repair these ravages of time?"

Mr. Sink explained that if you repaired, say, the roof, then the roof would outlast the rest of the building and some day you would have to repair the rest of it to keep up with the roof.

"You feel it would be cheaper to completely demolish the present structure and build a new one from the ground up?"

"In the long run, yes, sir," said Mr. Sink. "You get a uniform life expectancy."

One newly-elected member, a Mr. Win Sites, not yet broken in to the beauties of teamwork, asked if the metal parts of a new building wouldn't always have a greater life expectancy than the wooden parts. But Mr. Sink pointed out that rust could be as serious a problem as rot, and the traces were successfully got out from under Mr. Sites's belly.

The questioning went on until I had covered all my copy paper. Once Mr. Win Sites said, as if his ears were wanting to lie back again, "If the building was repaired, have you any idea what it would cost?"

"No, sir. I couldn't even give a guess without going into it more."

"Just a guess?"

"It might cost fifty thousand dollars. It might even cost a hundred and fifty. I couldn't tell."

"No more than a hundred and fifty?"

"I'd think it could be done for that."

We left these figures out of the story; they were just a guess, didn't mean anything. We worked the rest of it into a nice front page: a three-column cut of the roped-off entrance and a streamer above it, "COURT-HOUSE DECLARED UNSAFE." In the upper right we had, "COUNTY COUNCIL AT SPECIAL MEETING WARNED EDIFICE IN DANGER-OUS CONDITION—Repairs Not Practical—New Structure Discussed."—It was a nice layout.

. . . . Cousin Willy, as I say, hearing this heavy bombardment on his flank, sent an order to Ninety-eight to just take his shovel out of the car and stand by, while he sent out a reconnaissance unit to determine the nature of the firing.

2

The town took it like a man. Two or three people called in about it, but they were mostly just surprised and sorry; there was no suggestion of resistance. That's the wonderful thing about working in a Christian com-munity; they know they are sinners and they know that any news is going to be bad. Buildings crumble, rust corrupts, thieves break in and steal, and there is no health anywhere. Taxes are high and benefits are low; that's what the Bible says and that's just how things are in this world. You don't complain because that's the way, mysteriously enough, it was meant to be; if you watch your step you may get a better break at the next stop.

We half expected to hear from Cousin Willy, who didn't seem to be on the whole a very religious man, but there was nothing the next morning.

Ella Sue was the only person in the office when I got back from lunch and she seemed to have chips on all shoulders.

"So you're going to tear down the courthouse," she said.

I told her I had nothing to do with it.

"You could stop it if you wanted to."

"It's about to fall down anyhow."

"Worn out, eh?"

"You go down there sometime, if you don't believe it."

"How'd it get worn out so quick?"

"It's been worn out for years; they just discovered it."

"Who let it get worn out?"

"It just wore out."

"Why didn't you keep it repaired?"

"Listen, Ella Sue. What do you think I've got to do with it? I just tell the facts."

"You just tell some of the facts."

"Say!"

"Isn't it a fact they've already signed the contract to build a new courthouse?"

"I don't know anything about that."

"Well, you ought to know what's going on. Isn't that your job?"

"What's the matter with you today?" I said, getting pretty burnt up with this sort of holy attitude.

"I've got a slight case of moral indigestion, for one thing." She banged out two or three lines on the typewriter and tried to act as if I wasn't there.

"You don't understand," I said. "That old building's just tumbling down."

"Do you think every building that gets to be a hundred and thirty years old is tumbling down?"

"Certainly," I said.

"Well, your ignorance is just running away with you then.—There are buildings in Europe seven or eight hundred years old."

"How do you know? You've never seen them."

She burst into a rattle of typing and I left,—not having eased the normally strained relations between News and Society, and not caring if I hadn't.

. . . . The next afternoon the colonel opened up with a considerable armament. I didn't know how he

134

had got it into position because I hadn't seen any copy of his, but there it was.

It was disheartening,—disheartening in the same way as seeing a horse that you have just led out of a burning barn turn right round and trot back blithely into the flames.

He started out by describing the British forces taking to their ships from Savannah, "leaving behind them not the Colonies of the Crown but the United States of America." Then he switched inland to the little town of Fredericksville on the banks of the river, hardly anything left of it,—a few warehouses for storing furs and tobacco and presents for the Indians, a few houses left standing between the ashes and blackened beams of those the war had destroyed, the walls of the old fort hammered and splintered by the single six-pounder of the patriots who wouldn't stay licked.—"What did they do?" said Cousin Willy.

"One of the first things they did," he replied, "was to set aside a piece of ground on which to build themselves a school. The war formally ended in 1782; the charter granted for the establishment of the Academy of Habersham County bears the date 1783. Like sound practical men, they turned first of all to the future, to the minds of the children.

"And then they turned to the present, to preserving what they had, to law and order and the business of governing. The Citizens of Fredericksville—those namesakes of ours, for we are 'Citizens of Fredericksville' too—set aside 'a parcel of ground on a line with the Academy' and built themselves a courthouse; not the courthouse we know today, but one capable of growing into this one."

He described how "General George Washington, who, five miles below Fredericksville, had alighted from his carriage and mounted his horse," rode into the town and to the steps of the courthouse under the escort of the Independent Blues, the officials of the local government, "and a numerous cavalcade of respectable Citizens";—how the new windows in the face of the courthouse chattered to the salute of fifteen guns of Captain Howell's artillery posted at the old fort;—how General Washington "at half past four o'clock in the afternoon dined at the courthouse with a large number of Citizens" and lowered his eyes modestly to his crystal glass of Canary while a spokesman of the Citizens of Fredericksville presented to him an address of welcome:

"To the President of the United States of America," said the anonymous spokesman of the Citizens of Fredericksville, the manuscript of the address no doubt half lost under the elegant fringes of his best lace cuffs; "Sir, —Your journey to the southward being extended to the frontier of the Union, affords a fresh proof of your indefatigable zeal in the service of your country and equal attention and regard to all the Citizens of the United States. With these impressions the Citizens of Fredericksville present their congratulations upon your arrival here in health, with the assurance that it will be their greatest pleasure, during your stay with them, to testify the sincere affection they have for your person, their sense of obligation for your merits and for your services, and their entire confidence in you as the Chief Magistrate of their country. On your return, and at all times, their best wishes will accompany you, while they retain the hope that a life of virtue, benevolence, and patriotism may be long preserved for the benefit of the age, and the example of posterity."

How General Washington rose with a smile and thanked the Citizens of Fredericksville for "the favorable sentiments you are pleased to express towards me," and sincerely offered his best wishes for their "happiness, collectively and individually. I shall always retain," said General Washington, "the most pleasing remembrance of the polite and hospitable attention which I received in my tour through Georgia and during my stay in the residence of your government."

Cousin Willy added that General Washington did not speak long, being somewhat weary from his journey (though, as Cousin Willy pointed out, he was only fifty-nine), but lifted his glass in his right hand and, gazing out over them for a moment with his earnest eyes, said in a firm voice: "The State of Georgia and Prosperity to Fredericksville!"

Cousin Willy described the attendance of the President at "an examination of the pupils of the Academy," the satisfaction he "expressed at their proficiency" and his departure on Saturday morning,—"crossing the bridge over the river to the salutes of the Independent Blues and Captain Howell's Artillery."

He told of the visit of General Lafayette and his son some thirty years later, of the ceremony at the steamboat landing where he was welcomed first in English, then in French "on behalf of the French Citizens of Fredericksville," of the procession under the escort of "the Georgia Fencibles, Captain Holt, and the Independent Blues, Captain McKinne" again to the steps of the courthouse, where he was welcomed by His Honor the Mayor.

He described the visit of Daniel Webster, the visit of Henry Clay, "on a hot summer morning. Stripping to the waist in one of the courthouse rooms while a Negro brought him buckets of fresh water from the well in the courthouse yard, he washed and dried himself vigorously (he was only sixty-seven), put on a clean shirt and strode out upon the porch of the courthouse, from which he addressed the Citizens of Fredericksville."

"Are these the stones," cried Cousin Willy (completely oblivious to the fact that all this had nothing whatever to do with the present condition of the stones),—"are these the stones it is now proposed to level! These stones that have looked on Washington and Lafayette, on Webster and Clay,—this monument to our past, this embodiment of our common memories, this tablet on which we have engraved some chapters of our long story!

"The act itself," Cousin Willy concluded, "is unthinkable, but the mere suggestion of such a thing is indecent."

. . . . I felt like laughing out of a pure despair.

Mr. Hoats came in bearing with him an ominous silence. He sat down sideways in a chair and shook a cigarette out of a pack, not offering one to anybody. Dewey and I fumbled for matches; I even got to the point of having one lighted, but he coldly struck one of his own. He inhaled the smoke in a great preliminary heave.

"First of all, boys, I want it stopped. I don't care what excuse you give the old guy. And I don't care what excuse the old guy gives you. There's no excuse to justify a private citizen standing up and meddling in a lot of public affairs that don't concern him. Why, this man's interfering in the conduct of the government. He is trying to create dissension and trouble. It's practically sedition. You can't use the pages of the *Leader* for that."

Mr. Hoats stopped for a minute to draw on his cigarette again, and as if he had been waiting for that, Cousin Willy pushed back the door on its squeaking hinges and walked in.

Usually when somebody comes in, there is no greeting at all; we may look up, in the faint hope it may be the sheriff or someone equally newsworthy, but there is no "How-do-you-do." This time, though, I counted three voices raised in salutation: I said, "Good morning, sir"; Mr. Hoats said, "Hello there, Colonel"; Dewey groaned, "How are you?"

The colonel lifted his stick by the middle and touched the knob to his brim: "Gentlemen."

I saw Mr. Hoats crushing out his cigarette preparatory to leaving. I thought I might as well go too; there was no use in making it hard on both Dewey and Cousin Willy by staying.

"Take this chair, Colonel," said Mr. Hoats. "I'm just leaving."

"Keep your seat, sir," said Cousin Willy. "I can talk better standing up."

This brought what you might call a considerable silence.

There was not much answer to be made and I saw Mr. Hoats say to Dewey with a glance, "You've got your orders." I fumbled with a pint milk bottle half full of paste in order to give my superior the courtesy of the first chance at the door.

He was half way to the exit when Cousin Willy said, "Oh, Mr. Editor."

Mr. Hoats stopped with his hand on the doorknob.

"May I presume to ask," said Cousin Willy, "what

is the position of this newspaper in regard to the destruction of this fine old landmark?"

"Colonel," began Mr. Hoats patiently, releasing the doorknob.

"I am afraid you may have unintentionally created some question in the minds of the Citizens as to whether or not you intend to help them. I searched your pages last night for some word of condemnation of this plot; perhaps I overlooked it, but I could find nothing."

"I am afraid you don't understand, Colonel," Mr. Hoats said kindly. "The courthouse is in a dangerous condition—"

"But it can be repaired."

"I am afraid it is too far gone for that."

"Who says so, may I ask?"

"That is the report of the two best structural engineers in this section."

"The condition of the building," said Cousin Willy, "is very difficult to determine except by an entirely independent examiner,—preferably a man from out of town, a man who never heard of this courthouse." He put his stick under his arm and took a pace or two east and west. "Now when I was in the Canal Zone with Goethals, I had the privilege of seeing the great Miraflores Locks hewn out of the jungle, one of the greatest feats of skill in that entire monumental project. The man who was principally responsible for those great locks was a Captain Hickock (now Major), United States Army, Corps of Engineers. I knew him well. Major Hickock, it so happens, is now retired and living in Atlanta, Georgia. Let him look at this building. He will tell you whether it is falling down or not—"

"Colonel," said Mr. Hoats, "I don't doubt that your friend is an excellent engineer, and certainly nothing would give me more pleasure than to help in getting him this little job. But you can't ask the council to bring in a man from Atlanta on a very simple matter that our local engineers can easily handle. In the first place, no loyal citizen of Fredericksville wants to ask Atlanta anything, and in the second, the cost of bringing him here—"

"Hell's flood, sir! I'll get him here for nothing."

There was understandably no comfort in this promise for Mr. Hoats, after the last thing Cousin Willy had agreed to do for nothing; "He's not a practicing engineer, is he?"

"By no means. He is retired. It's nothing to him one way or the other."

"But, Colonel, you can't ask the County Council to accept an opinion of an engineer without a license. That would hardly be quite on the level."

"I don't care what the County Council does. This man can make a report for the information and guidance of the Citizens of Fredericksville."

"Any report he made would be open to criticism on the grounds of his not having a license."

"We will just offer it for what it may be worth."

"It would be a great mistake, Colonel. It implies a want of confidence in the government—"

"Now my suggestion," continued Cousin Willy, "and I have been discussing it with a number of responsible Citizens who all agree with me, is that the *Leader*, true to its name, should," he paused a minute to shape his right hand into a sort of mold, while we frankly held our three breaths in terror, "should sponsor a movement to call in an outside engineer—"

Mr. Hoats clapped his hand to his forehead.

"What responsible citizens have you been discussing it with?" Dewey asked him maliciously.

"They requested me not to mention their names," Cousin Willy replied innocently enough, as Dewey burst into an outright laugh.

144

I responded to his questioning stare by explaining to him hurriedly that it had come to be a joke round there how nobody would sign his name to any complaint.

"Well, these gentlemen will, never fear,—when the time is ripe."

We didn't want to argue the point; we had been round there a lot longer than he had.

But at the same time the idea struck me (and I imagine something like it had struck Mr. Hoats too because his spectacles seemed to have become slightly pensive) that there was a remote possibility that we might be approaching one of those occasional freaks in Fredericksville history when what used to be known as the "better element" among the citizenry was going to turn its attention for a few weeks to public affairs,—not with the least intention of doing anything about them, but more in the spirit of Mr. Hoats letting his eye travel harmlessly over the riant nudity beneath the plate glass on his desk. It was perfectly safe to assume there would be no real kicking over the traces, and if these citizens thought now they would enjoy being briefly tantalized with the vision of resistance, they too were our subscribers and maybe on the whole it would be simpler to let the colonel's protests crystallize the

145

resistance out of them than to call attention to it by removing the colonel from our pages and inviting the growth of the urge by damming it up.

Mr. Hoats, anyhow, seemed easier in his mind and I thought he might have begun at least to waver in his determination to dispense with Cousin Willy's services altogether. "I'm a newspaperman, Colonel, not an evangelist. My function is to inform our readers what is going on in the world, not to advise them what to do about it—"

"Of course you know better what your function is than I do," Cousin Willy pointed out, with a sort of delayed-action fuse.

"If there is a group of citizens that wants a third engineer to look at the courthouse, why,—bring him in. I will print the story. That's our position. And I am sure the councilmen feel the same way—"

"Just as you say, sir," said Cousin Willy, relieving the tension not only by the tone of his words but by removing his helmet and sitting down amongst us. "How do I get long distance on this telephone?"

Dewey, somewhat bewildered at the request but of course not suspecting any more than the rest of us the enormous call the colonel was about to put through, showed him which button to punch.

With this as a start, Cousin Willy telephoned "Major Anthony T. Hickock, United States Army, Corps of Engineers, retired, in Atlanta, Georgia," and we sat round there weak-legged on the weak-legged chairs, among the typewriters that with their bent and chipped and clogged bars turned out an erratic hieroglyphics that only a linotypist could decipher, among the hooks and the paste-bottles and the copy paper,—sat round there and silently heard Cousin Willy make a succinct date with his old friend to come down and examine the courthouse, no words wasted on either end, as if Cousin Willy were directing the major to take his battalion up to Bridge 21, send out his scouts, make an Estimate of the Situation, and await further orders. I thought I even detected a faint reminiscent glow at the colonel's jaw-bone, but I didn't pay much attention to it for the general sensation I had of sinking perceptibly deeper into whatever all this was turning out to be—

I could hardly believe my senses: here we had been in Fredericksville, going our way, our normal contented way, the government governing, the newspaper helping in any way it could, the citizens happy to have all that burden lifted from their shoulders,—everything going smoothly, everybody happy, minding his own business, living and letting live.

Then all of a sudden, Cousin Willy appears and begins to stir up dissatisfaction and bad feeling. It was the government's duty to name the squares; it was the government's duty to provide a county courthouse for the county to govern in, to see that the roof didn't fall in and kill a lot of citizens. The citizens had elected a government to look out for just that sort of thing, to take care of them. And now—

It was as if a well-connected aunt, for no reason in the world, went out in the kitchen one morning, told the faithful old cook who had raised her from a baby to go home, and started in frying the chicken herself.

CHAPTER VI

OBVIOUSLY the setup for foul play in the major's visit was practically perfect, and Mr. Hoats's nose for news was in hardly any respect keener than his nose for foul play; he had about as much faith in the over-all good intentions of humanity as a breathless fox. We didn't carry any build-up on Major Hickock's coming to Fredericksville, of course, but when he got there I was detailed to accompany him and the colonel on their tour of the building, partly as a reporter but also just to make sure they didn't go in a huddle and fling us a fast one.

And furthermore I was to be prepared, in case the major was lukewarm in his belief that the building could be repaired, to do half a column for Page Two on his failure to indorse the colonel's scheme.—Of course if the major agreed with the local contractors and declared it was impossible, I was going to Page One with a by-line.

I met them in the basement just after they arrived,

the major with his hands and pockets full of such things as a yardstick, a metal tape, a hammer, a steel square, a cold chisel, and a flashlight; the colonel was talking to Joe, the janitor, and incidentally transferring to him the greater part of the equipment.

The major was a stocky little man with a large head, his stiff white hair clipped in a military cut; his knee joints may not have been quite so elastic as at Miraflores, but the upper part of his body was erect and tight. He shook my hand with the tolerant grip of a broadminded warrior for a civilian, not saying anything but pausing courteously for a moment in his professional tapping of an interior wall with the butt of the cold chisel.

"Now, Joe," said Cousin Willy, "we want to see the courthouse, all the courthouse. I understand there have been cuts made in the floor and ceiling at sundry places."

Joe said there had been.

"Well, we want to see them, all of them."

The major was already round a corner, going at the building as if he were on a treasure hunt: "Main bearing walls all masonry," he flung back in a monotone, not seeming to care whether anybody heard him or not. "Plaster weak in spots."

Joe led us down the hall and pried up a rectangle that had been sawed out of the floor. The major creaked down on his knees and turned the flashlight inside; he opened his pocketknife and jabbed at some of the joists.

"Termites?" said Cousin Willy.

"Certainly not in any force," said the major.

I stuck my head into the opening. I didn't know anything about termites but I thought a decent interest might restrain any tendency in the major to exaggeration; it looked to me as if my chances of Page One might be fast getting ready to disappear.

Cousin Willy got down on his hands too. The whole arrangement, from a distance, no doubt looked deceptively like an informal game of dice; I don't mean to say that was why Councilman Wishum joined us. He may very likely have thought we were going to dynamite the building and wanted to make sure. But anyway, in a few minutes I saw a pair of glossless pink shoes beside us and I looked up into the councilman's puzzled frown. His silence was rather eloquent.

"Hello, Councilman," I said, standing up and giving him a wink. "These gentlemen are just checking over the building—"

But he cut me short. "If you're looking for where this old wreck is falling to pieces you can start over in that corner there." He nodded glumly at an array of black laths in the ceiling over the jury box in the City Court Room.

The major glanced at it. "Leak," said the major.

"I'll say it's a leak; the place is full of them.—Look at those bricks out there."

"Need pointing," said the major.

"Why, if one of those bricks fell out of there and hit somebody on the head—"

"But, my dear sir," said Cousin Willy, as if he hadn't heard me plainly address Mr. Wishum as "Councilman," "there is no necessity to throw the gun out with the spent cartridge."

I wished I could have crawled into the dark hole we had been looking at; for a taxpayer to use such a tone to one of the taxing authorities was like pinching a wildcat with your bare hands.

"I didn't catch your name, sir," said Mr. Wishum, as if he might be forced to resort to measures.

"I am Colonel W. Seaborn Effingham," said Cousin Willy, "United States Army, retired. May I present my friend, Major Anthony T. Hickock, United States Army, Corps of Engineers, retired. And this is my sister's boy—"

I suppose I almost shouted that the councilman and

I were old friends, but I don't know whether or not I was successful in blotting out Cousin Willy's genealogy.

Thankfully, Mr. Wishum didn't stay with us very long; he cast an indifferent gesture at some plaster cracks and exposed wiring, muttered "Fire trap," and soon left us, as if to our play.

Now about this time a very extraordinary thing began to happen. To make it clear, I must go back a little bit and try to explain about Ella Sue.

My attitude toward Ella Sue, though I had never stopped to give it much thought, was pretty much the attitude you would expect to find between News and Society. Frankly, all of us, at heart, resented Ella Sue. Old Miss Carrie Wilkes, her predecessor, had treated us all like bad boys, but her bad boys, and except for a water glass full of pansies or sweet peas or something like that, there wasn't much difference in the spirit of her office and of ours. Waste paper went on the floor where it belonged, and the five-cent paint brush sticking in the milk bottle of paste was hooked over the gummy rim with a paperclip, just as it was in our office.

There had been no smoking in Miss Carrie's office, but she would let you stand on the edge of the door sill and smoke, if you didn't let any part of the cigarette get more than half way past the door frame. We used to tease her by standing there smoking, inching farther and farther into the door, until the left side of her mouth began to get thin and her hand began to stretch out idly toward the water glass or a book the reprint houses had sent in for review or a box of pencils or what not; she once threw the paste bottle at Earl, who was a special pet of hers on account of being a stranger in a strange land, because he tried to get in with his cigarette by holding out in front of him the bribe of a fruit jar of white corn whiskey. That would have done it if anything could have, because the only thing the old lady liked better than corn whiskey was that very attractive concoction we know how to make in these parts out of our state fruit, called peach bounce.

One day Miss Carrie just up and got sick and died, and Earl and Dewey and I and Uncle Fun, the linotype operator who for decades had transposed her phonetic copy into unassailable orthography, together with two of the undertaker's henchmen (for she seemed to have no family left outside of the newspaper), lowered her into a very nice grave beside her illustrious forebears in an old corner of Wisteria Cemetery.

After she "left us," as we say, two or three ladies hurled themselves at the job. But they didn't like us very much, and what with our spontaneous but possibly, to a stranger's ears, not so engaging vulgarity, and the steps to be managed when the elevator wasn't running (which it usually wasn't), and such things, they didn't linger with us for very long.

I don't know what the qualifications are for handling the job, if any, but Ella Sue seemed to be making out; she must have been about twenty-five and she could take the stairs at a run and light a cigarette on the top one. I doubt if she had ever in her life swallowed peach bounce, but cigarettes she bought and smoked by the carton,—and padlocked them in her desk when she left the office. Yet we still had our inherited aversion to crossing the threshold with a lighted cigarette, even when seeing Ella Sue perched there behind a wedding or a garden-club luncheon with one in her mouth.

This curious shorting in the stimulus-response circuit of the Editorial Department probably tended to create in us newsmen a sort of mild psychosis in respect to Ella Sue,—that, and the fact that Miss Carrie's semi-maternal presence had failed to fortify us against having people with legs and figures round the office.

Unprepared as we were for this abrupt change of pace in the biological pulsations of the office, the simplest way out seemed to be to resent the whole thing, and this we did, maybe unconsciously at the time, and the few early gestures of friendship on the part of Ella Sue seemed only to stir up in us a tougher antagonism.

She made the business office paint her walls, put up Venetian blinds, lay a flowered linoleum on the floor; she even made them buy her a wastebasket. So when we discovered that she padlocked her cigarettes we just stopped going into the Society Office at all except on urgent business, and from the increasing silence which greeted Ella Sue's visits to us, it would have been apparent to most people that there was no real foundation for any lasting peace between us.

When Cousin Willy appeared on the field and she added to all these transgressions a sort of imperceptible smile at the very real embarrassments he began to cause us, added even a half-active, almost protective sympathy for him, it began to look as if he might become the rock that was to rend the *Leader* in twain. Because it must not be supposed that the importance to us of Society can be gauged by the size of its office force. The truth was, as we all silently realized, if necessity demanded that either the News Office or the Society

Office be closed up, the paper would last a good deal longer without news; on the slates of the Advertising Office where value is demonstrated beyond appeal, it is highly probable that Ella Sue had more stars in her crown than all seven of us put together.

Now the extraordinary thing that began to happen at the courthouse was this,—though I can see it is going to be difficult to present it in the exact combination of the sacred and profane that is its very essence, in exactly that intensity of light that reveals no material difference between an imp and a cherub.

We were examining the mortar in an interior wall, the major scratching out a little of the white dust with his knife, murmuring something about "No structural failure," when I felt somebody appear in the door at my right hand and looked round to see Ella Sue. She gave me a bright smile, tiptoeing in with an exaggerated care as if not to interrupt these weighty deliberations.

Now what in the world! I said to myself, and having been brought up on the Bible, I thought, And we may descend into the bowels of the earth and we are not alone for thou art there.

The possibility occurred to me that Mr. Hoats might be putting her in training to take over my beat; but then in a few minutes I thought I began to see it straighter: he hadn't sent her. Nobody had. She had come on her own,—possibly in the role of the ambitious cub reporter, headed for the city desk, always on the alert for his story, but it was far more likely, I thought, that she had come to check up on me and see that I didn't draw (and print) any wrong conclusions from the major's examination.

I thought the best thing to do under the circumstances was to pay no attention to her at all. This was easy enough except when it came to entering and leaving the rooms. Joe led the way, of course, and the major and Cousin Willy followed,—they were doing the work. But then came the gallery consisting of Ella Sue and me, and when we came to a door there was no way I could see of not handing her through first.

Except for those moments, ignoring her would have been easy. She didn't ask me any questions about what had gone on before she arrived; she didn't say anything, just walked about, listening and looking and keeping out of the way and making herself generally unexceptionable. She was not even overdressed, as Southern girls are so fond of being; some sort of outfit about equivalent to a man's weekday brown suit, though it was made of cotton and had a colored pattern and the skirt was fuller than there was any sense in. She carried a pocket book under her arm about the size of a solicitor-general's brief case, but she opened it neither for powder and lipstick nor for paper and pencil nor for cigarettes and matches. And so we proceeded about the building, Joe leading, I bringing up the rear. Her hat wasn't really big, but she had it stuck somehow on the back of her head in the prevailing style, so that following her round was like following a blind spot.

"I don't quite get," I said once to the blind spot, "how this old wreck makes the society column."

"Oh, I'm just here on my own."

"Curiosity, eh?"

"Interest."

We didn't go into it any further because at that point I heard the indefatigable major saying, "How do I get under the roof?"

Joe pulled out a bunch of keys and unlocked a narrow door that opened on a grimy stairway between the walls. "Mind yourself," he said and went up into the dark. The major and Cousin Willy followed at his heels as intent as if they had been on the scent of an enemy agent.

"You can wait right over there," I said to Ella Sue, possibly with some patronage, nodding at a chair.

"Can I?" she said, going to the bottom step.

"You won't find anybody socially prominent up there," I said.

But she didn't answer, what with probably not liking my tone, and obviously having the bit in her teeth anyhow.

By the time she started up the stairs, Joe had reached the roof and lifted aside a trapdoor, letting in a flood of sky-blue light. This made everything a lot easier because we could see what was ahead; I looked up politely past the apparently interminable seams of Ella Sue's half-silhouetted legs and saw Cousin Willy leaving the stairwell and, with an outmoded gallantry, holding out his hand to her.

In a minute we were all standing on a catwalk like the ones you see in pictures of the intestines of a dirigible; it had a railing along one side and led across the beams to a ladder going up into the clock tower, and off to one hand under the tower was a great pendulum oscillating slowly with a sly click at each end. It was warm up there but a nice wind was skirling round through the trapdoor.

The major swept his flashlight laconically about the beams and trusses. "Fire up here?" he said, pointing with the light at some black uprights.

"Way back just after the war," Joe said, "we had a fire up here."

"Confederate War?" Cousin Willy asked him.

"No, sir. Just the World War."

The major struck one of them with his hammer. I must admit it resounded like a new telephone pole. "Surface char," said the major.

He climbed over the railing and walked with simian agility along a double beam into the angle where the roof rested on the outside walls. In a minute he said, "Leak."

After a while he told Joe he wanted to go out on the roof. Joe led the way to the trapdoor, which was at the bottom of the slope, and through it out on to a flat gutter running along inside a high balustrade. Cousin Willy followed and as I started to move past Ella Sue to follow him, she said, "Give me a hand, will you?"

"You don't want to go out there," I said, "you'll ruin your clothes."

But she didn't even bother to answer. And right there, I think, was the turning point in my life. Never again did I feel the same toward Ella Sue,—or toward many other things, for that matter.

She stepped over the bottom of the trapdoor with

one foot, her right hand on my forearm and her left pressing down on the crown of her hat while the blue wind pasted the brim up. Then she stepped over with the other foot and let go of me in order to do something about her printed skirt, which was just about getting tangled up with her elbows.

"Oop! Sorry," she said.

I muttered something out of my subconscious, half falling off the catwalk with the shock of such a sudden intimacy.

When I recovered my footing I realized that it sort of annoyed me, for some reason, that Ella Sue's legs should have looked like that; there was something halfway impudent about them and at the same time something naive, and this didn't seem to fit in with the Ella Sue I had known before, which I had always considered mostly impudent. They had all the usual trappings of run-of-the-mill glamor, but what impressed you about them was not so much that, which practically comes in a tube, as something human and personal that was a little like discovering a patch of freckles on a movie star's nose. They ceased at once being merely legs and became Ella Sue's legs,—though I don't suppose there is any way of making the difference clearer to you than by mentioning the other annoyance that began to bother me, which was the thought that Ella Sue shouldn't have any better sense than to chase out into a wind like that, not caring who was behind her; it might just as well have been Hoats, for instance, as I.

The cold shudder that went down my spine at this hypothetical jealousy was, I reckon, as symptomatic of what was happening to me as the initial chill foretelling the approach of malaria, but my health had always been good and I paid it no mind. I guess the whole incident was a little like chancing to be conscious momentarily of the mosquito that bit you, though the fever itself may not appear for some time.

Anyway, I realized later that I should have known something was wrong, if only from the fact that, as we were leaving the building and I was summing up in my mind the indisputable conclusion that in the opinion of a major of engineers the courthouse was eminently reparable, I said to Ella Sue, "Want a dope?"

She said, "O.K.," and we stopped in Dunavant's on the way back to the office. It was a little queer to realize that, though I felt my acquaintance with Ella Sue had suddenly increased immeasurably, I still didn't know what her preference was in dopes: "I reckon you want a fountain dope," I said.

"Bottle," she said, though I suspect it was partly mere natural contrariness, because girls like Ella Sue almost invariably take fountain dopes,—and turn the straw round and round with their fingers just in front of their lips. Besides, it was clear enough in a minute that she didn't know how to drink out of a bottle. I didn't say anything; I guessed she might be really serious about her newspaper career and was determined to learn the profession from the bottle up, so to speak, taking the rough with the smooth, which I thought was a good attitude.

We were getting along fine,—talking about the courthouse, about how there was not much doubt about what the major thought, and so on. "Dewey ought to run your story on Page One," she said, giving me what I assumed to be a warm look.

"I reckon it will take up about two inches at the bottom of Page Five," I said modestly.

"It's an important story. You ought to have a by-line too—"

"No thank you!" I cried.

She studied me for a minute, then she said, "You mean you wouldn't want to identify yourself with opposing the gang?"

"They're no gang," I said. "If you didn't have them

to run the government for you, you wouldn't have any government. They're doing a public service—"

"I believe the phrase is 'rendering a public service'—"

And we were back almost where we had been before she climbed through the trapdoor,—almost, but not quite, because I couldn't seem to shrug off her opinion as easily as I used to could. In a few minutes we walked back rather silent to the office.

When I told Dewey the substance of what the major's report would have been, he just raised his eyebrows a couple of times.

"How much do you want on it?" I said.

"Skip it," said Dewey,—which was all right with me. I couldn't seem to remember much about it anyhow.

2

Of course we really expected Cousin Willy to give the incident complete coverage in the *Firing Line*.

But he didn't touch it. His next column he devoted to a description of the disheartened Georgia militia, camped under the pines in the late winter of 1781 at the investment of Fredericksville.

It was cold in the bottom lands, with fog wreaths

over the lagoons at reveille; they were "worn out with fatigue, in want of almost every necessary of life, and despairing of any speedy reinforcement from the army of General Greene." Colonel Brown and his regiment of British regulars seemed capable of holding Fort Frederick indefinitely, "and," said Cousin Willy, "this body of militia began to give themselves up to despondency and had formed the determination of abandoning their camp."

Major Jackson, alarmed but not showing it, called his adjutant and ordered him to assemble the militia in a great circle in front of the headquarters tent. Then Major Jackson ordered his horse saddled and brought to him; he could hear their mumbling voices as they gathered, shivering and hungry. Then he stepped boldly out of his tent and, mounting the horse, he drew his saber and addressed them.

He pointed out to them "the miseries they had endured, the cruelties and insults inflicted on their families by Brown and Grierson,—cruelties which their dispersion now would only tend to renew. 'Vengeance, lads,' said Major Jackson, rising in his stirrups, 'is now within your reach. To abandon the opportunity of obtaining it, is to abandon your pretensions to the character of brave soldiers and true men, is to sacrifice your feelings and duties as Citizens, as sons and fathers and husbands,—as Americans.'

"This plain and manly eloquence," Cousin Willy concluded, "was saluted with the acclamations of this gallant band of Georgians, who unanimously expressed a resolution to conquer or die on the ground they occupied."

Cousin Willy then turned away blandly to the situation at the Public Library. It looked as if he were giving us a war of nerves.

At first thought you might have believed there was no connection between the courthouse and the Public Library; beyond the fact that both were responsibilities of the local government and both were in something less than bounding health, there might have seemed but a scant relationship and the colonel might have appeared to be retiring his forces from the main theater, using the library in a rear-guard action to cover his withdrawal,—though, frankly, the extent of the concentration at the library might quite reasonably have aroused your suspicions.

The disposition of the forces deployed among the books, according to Cousin Willy's Estimate of the Situation as expressed in his own inimitable way in three or four columns, was this:

Not very many years after the Citizens of Fredericksville "had demonstrated their faith in the future of the town by establishing the Academy of Habersham County for the guidance of the young and the Habersham County Courthouse for the guidance of the adult," some ten or a dozen sons of the founders (among them one Albert Seaborn Effingham, though Cousin Willy modestly declined to mention that), gathered together and between them, in a moment of generosity probably following hard upon one of those occasionally fabulously worthwhile cotton crops that occurred in the South about once in a decade, contributed, somewhat in the spirit of their fathers, a sum for the founding of a library. It amounted to something like fifty thousand dollars.

I have never dared delve after the true reason for such a fantastic act. True, it was not a public library; you joined for a dollar or so a year, took out whatever books you wanted, and returned them sometime after everybody in the neighborhood had finished. But what I am getting at is, there was no profit in it for the founders; not by the wildest stretch of a promoter's imagination could the idea have been sold to a realistic businessman that here was an attractive investment. Yet they were all reasonable and responsible citizens,

168

well-to-do according to the lights of a little pre-Con-
federate War Southern town, all in their right minds
as far as can be ascertained at this date.—I don't know
why they did it. I reckon it is just one of those things
we have lost the key to, like the Etowah Mounds.

Cousin Willy, of course, took it that these were
hard-headed, practical men with reality enough to
invest in "that soundest of all projects, the minds of
the young people. Idealists," he digressed long enough
to point out, "are the really practical people. They are
the realists; not the materialists necessarily, but the
realists. Many who call themselves realists merely mean
that they are materialistic." He quoted those verses
about, "Here are enshrined the longing of great hearts
And noble things that tower above the tide, The magic
word that winged wonder starts, The garnered wis-
dom that has never died."

"A library is a graduate school," said he, and he
pictured these sons carrying on the traditions of their
fathers who had founded the Academy.

But anyhow, whether it was just in a moment of
weakness, or whether Cousin Willy's venerable fore-
bear had talked them into something, they put up their
money and endowed a library.

It struggled along somehow for three-quarters of a

century, subsisting partly on income, partly on contributions of this or that set of Voltaire, Goldsmith, Gib-
bon, and Scott; when the Academy was eventually
transferred to larger quarters, the library was moved,
appropriately enough, into the old Academy building.

The trouble was that a library supported by an income of two thousand dollars in 1925 was quite a
different proposition from one supported by two thousand dollars in 1850. So the trustees met and decided
to suggest to the local government that it take over the
library as a public institution, free to everyone, the
income from the endowment to continue of course but
to be supplemented by a grant from the government.

This suggestion, understandably enough, was about
as popular with the Home Folks as if the Trustees had
asked permission to stable a kind-hearted rhinoceros
in the Municipal Building. At the rate some other
Georgia cities were supporting their public libraries,
the government would have had to appropriate a mini-
mum of eight thousand dollars a year, which, the authorities were foresighted enough to realize, would
have such a demoralizing effect on the personnel of the
government that there might be trouble in finding
people to run for office.

The end of it all was that the government, public-spiritedly, did take it over and supplemented the two-thousand-dollar income by two thousand more practically taken out of their own pockets,—an act approaching in its almost whimsical generosity the inexplicable conduct of the founding fathers, for they simply handed back to the community two thousand dollars that the citizens had no right to have thought of again except as for ever lost.

Cousin Willy, though, was not satisfied. Instead of expressing any appreciation for this handout, or any sympathy with the personal sacrifices the government had to undergo by the loss of this money, he claimed that it was ridiculously inadequate. "Two and a half cents per capita," he cried, rising in his stirrups like Major Jackson, "when the normal appropriation for a public library in the South is fifty cents!"

He concluded his argument by taking the amazing position that without the endowment the government of Fredericksville would have had to put up the whole amount and that therefore the founders of the library, instead of endowing an institution for the culture and improvement of the Citizens, had merely endowed the government of Fredericksville.

It looked as if he were deliberately out to bring about the financial ruin of the Home Folks personnel, and their longsuffering and patience with him in all this is, I feel, a remarkable tribute to their genuine good nature.

. . . . Such, then, was more or less the lay of the land on the morning about ten days after the major had come and gone, when I stopped in at the courthouse and put to Mr. Jimmy Seats my usual inquiry as to what was cooking.

"The council," he said, "is going to call a public meeting to discuss the courthouse question."

I pushed my hat off my forehead.

He repeated what he had said word for word.

"But, Jimmy! How many came to the last public meeting,—counting you and me?"

"That's a long time ago, Al; it's hard to remember."

"Do you reckon there were fifteen?"

"It's not up to us to get the crowd. We just want to do what's right and proper and we want to find out the public's wishes."

"Well," I said, "what could be fairer than that?"

He clasped and unclasped his hands on the high desk. "This colonel of yours seems to be trying to give the impression that we're railroading this thing through. We want the public to get the straight of it." He gave me the date, about two weeks off, and wrote "8:00

P. M." on a pad with a very sharp pencil and flipped it at me.

"Here at the courthouse?"

"At the courthouse, in the Superior Court Room."

"You think that'll be big enough?"

"If it's not, we can move out on the front lawn."

I laughed, but Jimmy just concentrated on making a deep black period on the pad with his pencil point.

This seemed to me like the biggest piece of news that had come out of the courthouse since Henry Clay left. I hurried back to the office and told Dewey.

"What's got into them?" said Dewey coldly.

"It's a good idea," I said. "Let the public get it off its chest—"

"The public hasn't got anything on its chest!— Sometimes, lately, Al," he paused, shook his head, then went on patiently. "You're getting a new courthouse, Al. The plans are drawn. I've seen them with these eyes.—Gimme about three inches on it."

We ran it on Page Four under the head, "COUNTY COUNCIL TO HOLD MEET ON COURT-HOUSE ISSUE,"—which was such a gem of a half-statement I thought Dewey must have written it himself. It stood up there in front of my little piece like a detour sign.

CHAPTER VII

THE trouble with the colonel was that he seemed to have developed too great an admiration and respect for civil life, seemed almost to glamorize it, as civilians will occasionally glamorize life in the army, or landsmen life on the sea. This was human enough, Lord knows, since anyone is likely to look upon unexplored hills as necessarily the hiding place of the Grail, knowing full well the cache had not been in any country he has already trod,—but it may lead into difficulties. For, as a landsman may think of the "front end" or "rear end" of a ship, the colonel seemed to view all his new surroundings in terms of attack and defense, of "ours" and "theirs," of "enemy."

These people weren't "the enemy." They were just ordinary American citizens like everybody else, brought up with an almost superstitious regard for competition and pulling themselves up, in the good old American way, by any bootstraps they could find lying about unpulled. To throw yourself against them as if you were Sergeant Jasper springing into the musket balls whining over the fortifications at Savannah and raising the fallen flag, was a little silly. It seemed to me the colonel was, in reality, not so much Sergeant Jasper as a rabbit bouncing out of his nice brier patch and leaping across an open field under the muzzles of the twelve-gauge shotguns.

I said to him once, feeling strongly enough about it to risk sounding impertinent, "Colonel, sir," I said, "meaning no disrespect, but—but I hate to see you be a rabbit, sir."

He scowled at me uncomprehending through his blue-gray eyebrows.

"Yes, sir. I hate to see you headed lickety-split across this field for all these people to take free shots at you—"

But it didn't have any effect on him. "Thank you, Albert, for your advice," he replied, a slight sadness in his voice. "But it seems to me more like a rabbit to sit cowering in your nest."—And he continued on his course.

In truth, people seemed to think of him, less perhaps as a rabbit, than as a sort of captive dinosaur. Here was something that looked alarmingly like an honest man, and it more or less made the skin creep up at the back of your neck. It was a little like seeing preparations for smashing the atom: God knows what might happen. Integrity? Lord help our souls. . . .

Now most of our readers were successfully detoured round my story of the public meeting. But Cousin Willy read it,—read everything in it and a lot that wasn't. In fact, it seemed to suggest to his consciousness one of the most remarkable menageries of unicorns and griffons and sundry fabulous creatures that had ever failed to exist by land or sea or air. I read his account of what he saw, one evening in the Manhattan Café over my fried ham and hominy,—which therewith took up defensive positions under my belt that held their own throughout most of the night.

He saw the courthouse now, not as just a historic old building, but as a symbol of Law and Order and Democratic Procedure (all upper case), as a symbol of what we had fought the Revolution for, as representing a heritage of free government handed down to us over the perilous years which, through our carelessness and indifference, we had allowed to deteriorate until now something had to be done about it. Was it, like our Democracy, something to be repaired and altered to suit modern conditions, all the while preserving its structure and the grand simple lines of its exterior? Or was it to be knocked down and thrown out for something streamlined?

The courthouse was a symbol of the state of the world today, Cousin Willy went on, while my fried ham gently turned to rubber within me. It was in bad shape, granted; but it could be repaired. Who let it get in such bad shape? Why, the leaders, primarily. But the Citizens had let the leaders get in bad shape. Why didn't the Citizens complain when they saw it was needing paint and repairs? The war, cried Cousin Willy, is the struggle between the nations that want to repair what we have got and the nations that want to tear it all down for the national booty involved. The courthouse didn't represent an outmoded way of life; it represented law, which was not outmoded, and so forth and so forth. "This is the struggle, in miniature," Cousin Willy wound up in bold face, "that the Citizens of Fredericksville will decide next Thursday evening at the public meeting at the courthouse.—Take out your pencils, Citizens, and draw a circle round that date. It is mightily charged with tomorrow."

And to make everything even worse, as I waited at the cigar counter for Sadie to make my change, my eye fell on Mr. James Economy's wall calendar; the circle round the next Thursday was as big as the horn rims of Mr. Hoats's spectacles.

"What's that?" I said bitterly. "Are you having a holiday next Thursday?"

"Oh, don't you know?" Sadie began. But I grabbed my change and fled.

When I reached the office next morning, the whole piece was neatly clipped out and inserted in the roll of my typewriter, and Ella Sue was sitting innocently at her desk beyond the door frame, hammering out a wedding. I pulled it out by its neck.

"What's the matter?" she said.

"I don't like allegory," I told her.

"Maybe you like petitions."

"Petitions!"

"Do you want to sign a petition?"

Though still suffering from the initial effects of Ella Sue on the courthouse roof, I was sufficiently in possession of my senses to say I most emphatically did not. But I seemed to be no longer capable of simply going on with my business. "What sort of petition?" I asked her, walking to her office door and taking up a ridiculous posture, mostly on one leg.

She handed me a mimeographed sheet already half

covered with signatures, none of which, I suspected, was on file at any of the banks: "THE UNDER-SIGNED CITIZENS OF FREDERICKSVILLE RESPECTFULLY PETITION THE COUNTY COUNCIL TO DO EVERYTHING IN THEIR POWER TO PRESERVE THE COURTHOUSE BUILDING THROUGH EITHER REPAIR OR REMODELLING AND NOT TO DESTROY THIS FINE OLD LANDMARK."

"Do you think for a minute the County Council cares what a dozen citizens—"

"There are two hundred copies of that petition being circulated round town this morning. If each one has a dozen names, that's twenty-four hundred signatures."

"Yes," I said. "If each one has a dozen names that's twenty-four hundred signatures.—Ella Sue, you've reached the age of reason, do you really think free people in a free country are going to sign their commercial death warrant—"

"I'm not asking you to sign; I asked you if you wanted to sign." She held out a cool hand for the paper.

"Those people could have me put out of my job by tomorrow morning."

"Well, you don't want to sign, then. That's all I asked you; there's no pressure being brought to bear on you."

"I have nothing against the old courthouse," I said. "In fact I feel almost a personal attachment to it. But—"

"Just lay it there on my desk when you finish with it, will you?" she said, turning back to the typewriter and rushing through a deafening flutter of keys.

Such was the curious manacle that had been clamped upon my spirit by Ella Sue's windswept legs that, instead of loosening as the days had gone by, it seemed to be shackling me tighter and tighter, indeed seemed to be extending tributary tentacles this way and that, and I not only wanted to cast sanity to the dogs and sign that petition but I could even imagine myself taking a few copies of it and asking for signatures at the Municipal Building and even, Heaven help me, at the courthouse.

I managed to get out without doing any of that, but my footsteps were heavy at her displeasure. So that when Dewey sent me out on a story I was glad to be going, glad of the distraction.

. . . . The trouble was, the assignment was an interview with Captain Dresden Rampey of the local National Guard unit which had, strangely enough, just been issued two caliber-thirty machine guns. I went round to his office in the Waterworks Department at the Municipal Building and we had a talk.

He had a poster on his wall of a young man in a nice blue suit with wide yellow stripes down the pants and two or three stripes round his coat sleeve and a neat cap, striding along very pleased with everything, and it seemed to me, while listening at the same time to what Captain Rampey was saying, that if I had a suit like that Ella Sue's nose wouldn't be so up in the air, or if it was it wouldn't make any difference to me—

Anyhow, when I left that office I was a private in the Georgia National Guard.

2

I broke the news to Ella Sue the next night at the Sports Arena, just after I had bowled a long slow hook into a beautiful jangle of devastated pins. "By the way," I said, "did I tell you?"

"No," said Ella Sue.

I cast my voice into a casual tone: "I've offered my services to the government."

She lowered the big ball carefully back into the rack. "You've what?"

"You are now addressing Private Marbury of the Georgia National Guard."

I am modest enough, but I naturally thought she might blush a little with pride. But she only looked at me and said non-committally that she didn't understand.

"There's nothing to understand," I said. I beckoned to Pappy Daddy and told him to bring us a package of cigarettes.

"I think there's a great deal to understand."

"Why?—Democracy is threatened; I reach for my gun. Not to sound melodramatic, but it's as simple as that."

She picked up the ball again and balanced it by her cheek, gazing at me in a way that, with the most conservative intentions in the world, I couldn't help interpreting as something between concern and admiration. She didn't seem upset at all, though, because her ball struck the head pin just to the right of center and swept the alley as clean as a new broom.

"It seems funny to me," she said, "that you should be so much more concerned about Democracy in Europe than Democracy in Fredericksville."

"My dear girl," I said, amazed at her. "What happens in Europe is directly connected with what happens in

Fredericksville. You can't isolate our town and think we can forget Europe—"

"Neither can you isolate Europe and forget Fredericksville. And as long as Fredericksville is right under your hand and Europe is three thousand miles away, it seems natural to think you might first give a thought to Fredericksville."

I began to see what the drift was then.

"I should say, in the affairs of Fredericksville, you were quite an isolationist, no?" She was obviously getting her foot into the stirrup.

"Listen, Ella Sue—"

"I don't see how you get to be such an interventionist in the affairs of Europe."

"It's not the affairs of Europe. It's our concern."

"But why is it more our concern than the affairs of Fredericksville?"

"Oh, it's bigger, it's more important. Women don't understand—"

"I don't mind intervention but I don't see why intervention shouldn't begin at home."

I rolled a fast one but it only took off the back corner. "You don't think anybody ought to join the National Guard until he has made everything beautiful in his home town—"

"I think he would make a lot more sense if he tried when he could."

It was all pretty maddening. The argument went on all the way back to her front porch, but nothing I could say seemed to make her see that here was something bigger than Fredericksville. "Hell," I finally said in exasperation, "I'll sign the petition."

"I'm sorry," she said, "but I'm afraid there's no more room on the paper—"

If ever anything had turned to ashes in a man's mouth it was that enlistment. Of course the duties were not too severe; we only drilled a couple of hours a week, which was all right if it didn't get any worse. But she had undermined the whole structure of it; it had been my understanding that women were still patriotic enough to want a man in uniform, and though my uniform turned out to be only a khaki shirt and pants such as you can buy off the "working clothes" tables in Penney's and gave me in general more the appearance of a filling-station operator than a warrior, still I had thought any girl as perspicacious as Ella Sue would see the difference.—To say now that I was sorry I had gone to all that trouble for nothing, would be putting it mildly. In fact, I went so far, at our next drill, to mention the possibility of resigning to our

Sergeant Bushrod (vulgarly known as "Sweetie Pie"), but he was even more unsympathetic in his common way than Ella Sue.

. . . . Fortunately a little incident happened at my fourth drill that took some of the sting out of my predicament.

For the first few evenings I had been too busy trying to get my muscles into a military frame of mind to give much concern to anything beyond the tension that seemed to be developing between me and Sergeant Sweetie Pie, but during the occasional rest periods I did have time to glance furtively about the field at the other units and the officers standing around.

I knew most of them, of course, from my contacts with the Municipal Building-Courthouse personnel; naturally, the Governor couldn't turn the Guard over to a lot of raw citizens he didn't know anything about. Among the few I didn't recognize, I noticed one who seemed to stand a little apart from the others, as if observing the training from a distance, to get the picture as a whole, his hands behind him. I thought, in fact, from his attitude, he must be the boss of the whole thing, though the regular officers didn't seem to pay him much notice. I didn't pay him much, either, beyond realizing casually that he was always there under a sort of Oglethorpe Oak when I arrived and was still on the field when I left.

One August night it was particularly hot, though the sun had sunk behind a murderous-looking cloud in the west. We went on with our drill; our lieutenant was not there, but Sergeant Sweetie Pie most emphatically was, and he had the sweat rolling down our pants legs by the time the storm broke.

It caught us over in a far corner of the drill ground, with lightning and sudden tumbling thunder and snapping sheets of rain that sent any unattached officers running for the school building. Sweetie Pie seemed undecided for a minute whether to take us in or continue as if nothing was happening, but the assembly whistle reached us from the porch of the school and we turned back on the double.

Half way across the field we overtook the lone officer, the rain pasting his wet shirt against his shoulders, his trousers stained black; he halted as we came closer and watched us approach, paying no more attention to the storm than if it had been a southwest breeze.

As we came abreast of him, Sweetie Pie slowed us down to a walk and saluted, and I saw, of course, that it was Cousin Willy. He drew himself up and answered the salute as if we had been marching past in review, not with the vim of a junior officer but still with every detail machine-cut and easily right, the drops of rain dangling on the visor of his cap, little rivulets running down his straight wrist and up his sleeve.

I didn't think he saw me but evidently he did, because when we were dismissed he walked over. I gave my salute everything that was in the book and maybe a few extra touches of my own, our relationship being now that of ranking officer and recruit; he returned it with a smile and held out his wet hand.

"Congratulations, my boy," he said. "You have committed an overt act in behalf of your country and I am proud of you."

I am glad to say I blushed slightly under my rainwater, understanding my motives better than he did. But I felt impartially that his approval was no more unjustified than Ella Sue's disapproval, and it served to cancel out some of my hurt.

"You are the commanding officer here, sir?" I said, too intimately but being still six-sevenths civilian.

"Oh," he laughed, "by no means."

"I've seen you here every drill—"

"When the old fire horse smells smoke, you know,"

he smiled, brushing some of the water out of his moustache. "Report back to barracks and change your uniform. Dry your leather slowly and apply a little neat's foot oil when it dries—"

CHAPTER VIII

THE thing about Cousin Willy was that, for some reason or other, it was so hard to feel really certain whether you were seeing through Cousin Willy or Cousin Willy was seeing through you. He had a column about this time describing the death of the sixteen Georgia militiamen in the retaking of Fort Frederick from the British; it seemed perfectly innocent, and maybe it was.

He told of the Americans preparing to assault the fort, digging the oblique approach trenches toward the walls with picks and shovels collected from the plantations round about, under the constant sniping of the four hundred British soldiers inside the stockade. Eight of the militia were wounded as they lifted their shoulders to throw out the Georgia sand; three were shot diagonally through the head and died instantly. "But the besiegers," said Cousin Willy, "held to their task and the works progressed with commendable rapidity."

He digressed (if it was a digression) long enough to describe one Captain Rudolph, "a fair-haired youngster of twenty-nine, whose grandfather was one of the persecuted Salzburgers who had come to Georgia in the winter of 1734 in search of freedom. The captain was himself a native of Fredericksville and when, on the twenty-eighth of May, at midnight, a detachment of the enemy fell with great vigor upon the American works in the river quarter, he requested of Colonel Lee the honor of throwing them out, for though he had inherited from his parents a great love of peace, he had inherited also no less a love of freedom and he did not take at all kindly to the occupation of his birthplace by the forces of tyranny." Colonel Lee, whom Cousin Willy pictured as a "most understanding gentleman," granted his request. "For a long time," said Cousin Willy, "the struggle was continued with mutual pertinacity till at length Captain Rudolph, by a combined charge, with the bayonet cleared the trenches and drove the enemy with loss into his stronghold.—Casualties among the militia were necessarily heavy: there were five dead and twelve wounded."

In the American camp, Cousin Willy continued, "the only reliable field-piece was an old six-pounder, useless for opening a breach in the scarp and, on account of its flat trajectory, valueless for the harassment of the enemy within. It was therefore deemed proper to construct a tower on which the piece could be elevated sufficiently to cast its projectiles within the fort, and orders were issued for cutting and transporting the necessary timber."

All day the Georgians toiled, "felling the mast-straight pines," dragging them through the brush. On the night of the thirtieth, "while one weary company raised the timbers, bleeding rosin (for it was May), lashed the crossties, braced the interior with fascines, earth, stone, brick, another company as weary as the first, threw up a protective bank of loose sand and clay on the side toward the fort to preserve the tower when the enemy opened on it with his eighteen-pounders in the morning."

But the enemy, observing what was going forward, made a midnight sortie "with the strength of his garrison" in a desperate attempt to destroy the tower. "In anticipation of just such a move, however, the lines in that quarter had been doubly manned, and Rudolph's infantry was conveniently posted in support. Although the action entailed the loss of seven killed and twenty-two wounded, the sortie was eventually repulsed about two-fifteen in the morning."

The sun was hardly clearing the tops of the Carolina forests when the enemy opened fire on the tower with two of his heaviest pieces of ordnance. "Regardless of this annoyance," Cousin Willy remarked with a proper pride, "the builders continued their labors."

On the first of June the tower was completed and during the night the six-pounder was hauled into position on top of it. Throughout the next day it raked the interior of the fort, "commanding it entirely, with the exception of the segment nearest the tower and a few points sheltered by traverses. But when at nightfall Colonel Brown was invited to surrender his only reply was, 'It is my duty, as it is also my inclination, to defend this post to the last extremity.' "

So during the night an ample supply of powder and shot were transported to the tower and the Georgians were posted in the assault trenches,—"pleased," in Cousin Willy's words, "that the time was near which would close with success their severe toils."

And the time was indeed near. For at daybreak, before the advance was ordered, "an officer with a flag was seen approaching from Fort Frederick."

"On the fifth of June, 1781, at twelve o'clock," Cousin Willy concluded, "the British garrison, some three hundred strong, marched out of the west gate with shouldered arms and drums beating to a place agreed on, where they piled their arms. In acknowledgment of his part in the action and of his being a native of the town, the fort was delivered up to Captain Rudolph, who took possession with a detachment of the Georgia Legion,—and Fredericksville was once more in the hands of its people—"

. . . . It all seemed innocent enough, Heaven knows. It was just that you somehow couldn't quite tell whether Cousin Willy knew the rules or not. It seems absurd not to be able to tell, but you couldn't quite tell.

Even the Home Folks lawyers, who made the rules, were at heart a little perplexed. For, so square-shouldered and unfaltering was Cousin Willy's attitude that it inevitably suggested to you the suspicion that, if he didn't happen to know your rules, he knew some others that you didn't know and that were just as good,—or possibly better. And the strange part of it all was that even the lawyers seemed at heart inclined to be puzzled. They had had education enough, I reckon, to realize that after all there was a good deal in law they didn't know, and perhaps they wondered a little if possibly Cousin Willy's strange point of view might have evolved out of that murky region.

The truth was, I suspect, they were a little super-stitious about Cousin Willy. Even among the sharp-ers, there was undoubtedly the realization (for they were practical men) that after all the Fredericksville Municipal Building was but one of thousands and that somewhere higher up in the realms of government there were mightier men than they, and I firmly believe that occasionally, perhaps in that nebulous moment between sleeping and waking, the half-formed possibility assailed them that, in the words of the Book, maybe this was he of whom the prophets had told.

They were zealous churchmen; they perhaps re-garded the church (cannily, for there was nothing ro-mantic about them) as more of a hedge against some possible cosmic inflation than as a sanctuary of the spirit, but they passed the plate on the Sabbath and groaned an understanding "Amen" under many a Bap-tist dome and Methodist spire, and being convinced it had happened once, they could never be really com-fortable in their minds that it might not happen again. —I am not talking about their conscious thoughts; I am talking about those nebulous moments and those nebulous shapes in the realm their thoughts came from. Consciously, they would have decried such a thing, even with indignation or outright wrath at the sacrilege; but in that other realm I suspect they were not absolutely sure.

Cousin Willy bothered them; they felt like giving their heads a quick shake to see if it changed anything. They were as mildly upset by him as you or I would be if we suddenly encountered someone who would not accept payment in gold or silver but preferred to transact business with peanuts or old Virginia hams. If he were alone in this preference, we should put him down, of course, as merely crazy; but if he had the backing of, say, Clyde Manadue, who you knew could not be crazy,—well, we should begin to get a little balled up.

Superstition was what it was. You may not believe in ghosts, and yet after a few hours alone in an empty house with wind and rain and maybe a mouse or a trapped squirrel, your fine disbelief loses some of its edge. You still don't believe in ghosts, of course, but you don't disbelieve in them quite as strongly as you did.

Some of the authorities got just plain mad; they stomped their feet and cursed him a little among themselves. Others, the more outstanding realists, went down to the Assessor's Office to see if there wasn't some way of getting all this down to rock bottom; the only thing they found, of course, was a little five-acre piece of real estate in the county and a six-hundred-dollar automobile. Some thought of objecting to his unwarranted interference in public matters on the grounds of his having no right to speak since he had no property in the city; others thought of raising his water bill, others of lowering it, and others, the men of law, just sat tight and bided their time for a spell, watching, as lawyers will, out of a corner of the eye.

Some had still a different plan, and one morning after Cousin Willy had told his readers for the third time to "put a ring round that date," he had a telephone call from his old pal, Clyde Manadue. "Will," said Mr. Manadue, "I've got a little matter I want to talk to you about sometime. Can you meet me down at the library for a few minutes any time the next day or two?"

Cousin Willy inspected his blank engagement pad and told him he could meet him down there in about fifteen minutes. They settled on six o'clock.

And as the courthouse clock began to strike the first note of the hour, the colonel, as if arriving on the field to take a regimental review, stepped out of his car and marched up to the crenelated library. Fifteen minutes later Mr. E. O. Sandifer, president of the library, arrived and five minutes after that, Mr. Clyde Manadue. "Come out and see our roses," said Mr. Manadue, leading Cousin Willy along by the hand he was shaking, his love of the beautiful sweeping all before it and leaving him powerless to proceed to business until the cries of the artist in him had been somewhat stilled; he led them out into the court and leisurely called the roll of all the buds and blossoms, chucking two or three of them platonically under the chin.

Cousin Willy tried to recall Clyde's exact words over the telephone; he was just about to decide that he had misheard him when Mr. Manadue said, "Well, suppose we begin?" and adjourned them to the directors' room.

When they were all seated, Mr. Manadue folded his hands on the table between them. "First of all, Will," he said, "I want to thank you on behalf of the trustees for your interest in the library—"

"Not at all," said Cousin Willy. "Every human being is interested in a public library. A library is a chock under the wheel of progress; you can't slip back so easy if you've got a library behind you."

"Exactly," said Mr. Manadue indulgently, as if Cousin Willy had whisked the words right out of his teeth. "Now we've been trying for years, Will, as you know, to get enough money from the local governments to do a little painting and repair work. It has been uphill all the way."

Mr. Sandifer shook his head as if his climbing muscles still ached.

"There is now a chance, however," Mr. Manadue added more brightly, "that something may come of it."

"Good," said Cousin Willy.

"Thanks to you," he put in generously, giving Cousin Willy a warm glance.

"I am very glad," Cousin Willy began.

"The situation is this." He raised and lowered his clasped hands a couple of times. "The other day at the bank, Sandifer, here, and I were talking to a member of the Library Board. I am not free to mention his name—for obvious reasons."

The reasons were far from obvious to Cousin Willy but he didn't see that the member's name made any difference anyway.

"This member of the Board had just come from talking to some of the, the 'powers that be,' and he was most delighted to have found them very cooperative."

"Splendid," said Cousin Willy.

"Now I've been round a long time, Will. I'm a practical man. I can see through the eye of a needle," he nodded his head two or three times. "It is my personal belief that the government can be induced to spend twenty thousand dollars on a general repair and rehabilitation of the library."

"Bravo!" said the colonel.

"And not only that," said Mr. Manadue, warming with the approval. "Twenty thousand dollars alone would put the building in first-class condition, give us adequate lighting, new stacks for all the books we at present have to keep upstairs in storage cases, a new reading room—"

"Wonderful!"

"But in addition to all that, there is reason to think they would be able to obtain a grant from the WPA." He took a silver pencil out of an inside pocket at the approach of all these figures and coaxed out the lead as you might take the "safety" off your pistol. "A grant from the WPA of the usual one-third would bring the total value of the improvements up to some twenty-seven thousand dollars." He wrote the amount on a pad and showed it to Cousin Willy. "It is the opportunity we have been working for all these years."

"What got into them?" said Cousin Willy innocently.

Mr. Manadue smiled a little at the president, then at his pencil. "Of course they couldn't offer to cooperate with us like this without naturally expecting some cooperation in return—"

"Improving the library is not cooperating with us any more than with themselves—"

"The proposition that was discussed with the member of the Board amounts to this: I believe they will agree to spend twenty thousand dollars on the library, supplemented by whatever WPA grant they can obtain—seven, eight, or ten thousand dollars—on one condition." Mr. Manadue looked at Cousin Willy and Mr. Sandifer looked out of the window at the star-shaped leaves on a sweetgum tree.

"The proposition of repairing the old courthouse over there is both impractical and undesirable. Plans have been drawn for a fine new building, specifications are about to be let; to try to prevent it is simply hopeless, simply a waste of time. The proposition, frankly (and I believe in being frank), is that I believe they will donate this twenty thousand dollars to the library on the condition," he smiled, "that the writer of '*On the Firing Line*' drop the courthouse contro-

versy and temper his criticisms of the government with
a little more mercy."

"Well!" said Cousin Willy, while a mocking bird
piped a warm song into the sudden silence.

"Temper his criticisms with a little more reality,"
Mr. Manadue added, throwing a temporary sort of
bridge across the yawning quiet as the effect of the
proposition on Cousin Willy seemed for the moment
undeterminable. "That is essentially the suggestion, as
you understand it, isn't it, Sandy?" he asked the president after a minute.

"That's my understanding of it, yes, sir."

"The thing about it is, Will," he continued, "the
old courthouse is gone. Whatever the right and wrong
of it was—and many people don't agree with you that
the building could be preserved, or should be, for that
matter—that's over the dam. There is no way of saving the courthouse. That is the hopeless position we
are in. Now here comes along a chance to save something out of the wreckage; there is nothing to gain by
continuing the controversy, while by ending it, the
library gets the improvements it needs so—"

"Of course I couldn't do that, Clyde," said Cousin
Willy regretfully, "but—"

Mr. Manadue interrupted him hastily; "Don't give

an answer on it now, Will. Just turn it over in your mind. It looks like there is everything to gain and nothing to lose—"

"It isn't so much this building," said Cousin Willy. "That is important, but what is more important is that the wishes of the Citizens should be paramount."

"But it isn't up to the citizens to decide these delicate questions directly, Will. That's not according to the principles of representative government. The citizens elect their representatives and the representatives decide. If the citizens don't like the decision, next time they just elect different representatives."

"The Citizens have a constitutional right," said Cousin Willy, "to petition for redress of their grievances—"

"But, Will,—"

"It is important for them to exercise that right often enough to realize they have it. In the early days we petitioned the King. He paid no attention, so we had to take things into our own hands—"

"You think it over, Will, and call me in the next few days,—or let me call you. What's your number?"

"There's no use in thinking it over, Clyde," said

Cousin Willy sadly, as if the proposition was a four-mile run and he knew his limitations. "I couldn't possibly do it."

Mr. Manadue bumped the rubber of his silver pencil two or three times lightly on the table.

"Maybe I could have done it once in my early youth, I don't know; I did some pretty fool things. But now I am getting to be an old man, and it seems to me one of the great compensations for getting old is that you can talk,—you can speak freely. There's no longer any use in holding it back; there's no point in saving it until one day you find you're stuck with it." Cousin Willy looked at them both with a pleasant smile, but they were solemn. "If an old man doesn't speak his mind, what compensation does he have?"

"I am sorry you won't see this thing realistically, Will," said Mr. Manadue. "Idealism is all right in its place, but—" He got to his feet, no more interested in finishing his sentence than in throwing good money after bad. He put away his pencil and, since a terminal silence seemed to have fallen on the room, he turned up both palms of his hands in a little gesture and glanced at Mr. Sandifer.

"Idealism is everything, Clyde," said Cousin Willy

in that tone. "Without it you go stumbling along in the dark from day to day. It's your match in the dark tower—"

"Romantic, then. Whatever you want to call it.—Come on, Sandifer."

"There is nothing more romantic in any of us than to think we are not," said Cousin Willy, turning away to the sweetgum tree. "We are such stuff as dreams are made on—"

His old friend walked coldly out of the room and he sat down again by the table.

. . . . After a while, there was a knock at the door and Ninety-eight looked in quizzically with his chauffeur's cap in his hand: "Mr. Colonel, sir?"

The colonel frowned at him. Then he said, "All right, orderly." He pulled himself together, got up and followed him.

CHAPTER IX

THE colonel took this attitude of his friend pretty much as his Grandfather Elias had taken the Yankee ball in his left forearm at Fish-dam Bluff; in the press of the action, he had no time to give it much consideration. It was painful and most unfortunate, but the enemy was still maintaining his lodgment on the bluff and the main assault was only about to begin. If he sensed any wariness in the greetings of his old pals as he went about the streets, any inclination in them to take advantage of the great width of our sidewalks, he gave no indication of it; and maybe it was not apparent, though I did get the feeling, along about this time, that a general impression was beginning to work among the more responsible elements of our town that the colonel was perhaps not wholly to be relied on.

But other things were in the air—

I walked into the courthouse grounds about fifteen

minutes before the meeting. The picture was just about as I had imagined it: six or eight cars of more or less eroded chic parked at the curb, two or three groups of women in the sterile garb common to maiden aunts and widows passing in under the light of the old iron lanterns that flanked the entrance. A few men were standing round outside as if it were church and they were holding the usual manly vigil until the sermon began, Mr. Alsobrook, the government attorney, pulling comfortably on a thin, after-supper cigar, Commissioner Pettle beside him in the shadow checking roughly those hardy non-communicants who were coming to the meeting.

I stopped beside three young fellows whose faces I knew, though I couldn't remember their names. One of them had read copy for us for a couple of weeks once until something better turned up on WPA; he was the last person in the world I should have expected to care whether the courthouse rose or fell. "What are you doing down here?" I said.

"It's a public meeting, isn't it?" he grinned without opening his lips. "And anyhow, we're invited."

"Well, that's fine," I said, wondering where Cousin Willy could possibly have encountered this skate. I was a little surprised to see that Cousin Willy had his feet near enough to the ground to realize the desirability of having a reliable nucleus to the meeting, but things were rapidly getting to such a state that the only way the colonel could really surprise me was by suddenly reverting to my original idea of him.

I talked to them for a minute or two, then I told them I reckoned I would go on in. "You all not worried about getting seats?" They were not very quick on the smile, feeble jest though it was.

When I got to the side door of the old brown courtroom with its triple-height ceiling and its chandeliers and its ponderous, rubbed railings swooping up and down in a way that reminded you of the ball-racks at the bowling alley and the high-backed swivel chairs where a juryman might rest his heavy head of a summer afternoon, the whole place permeated by a faint odor of disinfectant that was after all not inappropriate to cleansing justice,—when I got to the door I was stopped by a considerable shock. All the chairs in the witness box were taken and most of the three front rows of spectators' seats. The chairs for the jury were all occupied, largely by government officials,—those with any legal training amiably rocking, as if all this were in about the category of a Second Ward barbecue; those whose more simple instincts had never received a legal disciplining seemed to be frankly keeping the corners of their eyes bearing, and without any pretense of contentment, on the main entrance.

Things were obviously not moving in any too happy a direction. It was only five minutes to eight by the great clock and pendulum behind the judge's throne and there were not only already something near a hundred people seated in the room but they were pouring in the double doorway, a good many of them with a sheet of paper in their hand. I caught sight of Cousin Willy's pink dome near the door, where he stood like Saint Peter welcoming a congregation of Methodists who, by some mundane catastrophe, were arriving all at once. They were mostly, as I say, widows with annuities, or sisters and aunts with an equally sound misunderstanding of trade and finance.

I spoke to Aunt Lulu, whom I hadn't seen since Cousin Anna died.

"Where's Uncle Amos?" I said with some malice, knowing that Uncle Amos's retainer from the bus company prevented his getting down off the fence as effectively as if it had been a prong of barbed wire hooked into the seat of his pants.

"Your Uncle Amos had to go up to Chatham County on business."

"Oh, that's too bad, isn't it? I trust he got a chance to sign the petition before—"

"He wanted to sign it, but he got away in such a hurry—"

"Goodness gracious!" I said.

I asked Sally Manadue where her papa was. He had gone in the other direction, toward Thunderbolt. The president of the Broad Street Association was in bed with a horrible cold, and the heads of the civic clubs were all detained at meetings and conferences here and there about the county. The only males I could recognize were Jim Economy and his brother Louis, Lim Wong who owned a grocery store in the Territory, an Italian cabinet-maker named Celli, an old man with a white goatee named Eisenschiml who specialized in gravestones, and a tall figure with familiar-looking gentle eyes whom I couldn't place at once but later identified as Cousin Albert who ran the grocery store near the colored cemetery,—and of course the three young men of the claque that I presumed Cousin Willy, in a moment of actually brushing the earth with his toes, had persuaded to lend, or possibly rent, its influence.

There may have been a few others. They were coming in so fast now I couldn't keep an accurate count, what with sympathizing with the understandable cloud on the faces of the government and trying to determine what Ella Sue could possibly find interesting in a nearsighted teacher of English literature at the Academy, named Bland.

The whole thing was interrupted by three or four slow whacks (in about the cadence you would brake a car that was getting too much headway) on the kitchen table where learned counsel usually piled its brief cases but which was occupied now by the chair and a clerk; it was after eight by the clock, though there were still people trying to get in the door past the little group round Cousin Willy, borrowing pencils and looking for places to rest the petition while they signed their reckless names.

"The meeting will please come to order," said the chair, a round little man by the name of Jeffie who somehow always gave you the impression of standing largely on his heels; he handed the table another pair of thumps.

I found myself a railing to lean on and pulled out my handful of copy paper. Meetings weren't usually started in our trade area before twenty minutes past the hour, but this promptness suited me fine because, as I whispered to Councilman Wishum, the sooner we

210

started the more chance we had of getting out of the place before it collapsed.

The chair rapped again. But before he could repeat his request for order, a familiar voice rose above the vestiges of confusion: "Just a minute, Mr. Chairman, sir, if you please; these ladies haven't yet found seats."

The result of this little remark struck me as being characteristic of that whole summer; the momentary effect was a decided weakening of the government's position, but whether Cousin Willy was ingenious enough to have planned it that way or whether the Lord just so directed it in a sort of appreciation for a great innocence, I don't know and I don't reckon I ever shall know.

Anyhow, the chair saw what was happening and grabbed hold of the situation just before it was snatched out of his hands by pointing the handle of the gavel and saying in a not-to-be-outdone graciousness, "Ladies, I believe you will find some seats over in the corner there under the window," and waited for a minute with his courteous finger tips on the table. Then he said, "I know you are all anxious to get through here and go on about your own affairs and I won't keep you any longer than necessary—"

"On the contrary, sir," began Cousin Willy, but

there was some applause from back in the middle of the gallery for no very clear reason that I could see, and Cousin Willy thankfully didn't elucidate.

The chair continued: "We invited you here tonight, ladies and gentlemen, to express any opinions you may have on the disposition of this old building. As you know, parts of it were built over a hundred and fifty years ago and we can't expect anything to last for ever. —First, let me express our appreciation of your splendid interest in attending here tonight; it is very gratifying to see even this small percent of the total population. Don't be afraid to speak up; we want your ideas. Of course we can't promise to necessarily follow your suggestions. We are concerned with the desires of eighty thousand people and this assembly numbers perhaps,—five hundred?"

He glanced down at the clerk for his estimate which, from the shake of his head, must have been considerably lower. "Well, say, five hundred," continued the chair, declining the benefit of the doubt, "a little more than half of one percent. Naturally we must be careful not to give undue weight, in a democracy like ours, to any minority. But we want you to express yourselves and we are here to listen and to answer questions.—Now, in order to acquaint you with the dangerous condition of the building, I am going to first ask the clerk to read you the reports of the two independent contractors who have examined it."

The clerk adjusted his glasses and read the reports; I didn't pay much attention because I had heard them before, but they went into the walls, the floors, the roof, the wiring, the plumbing, and all the rest. Obviously, the place was a shambles. "In the light of all these circumstances," the final report concluded somewhat wistfully, "it is to be hoped that the commission can find a way to erect a new building which will save the county money and obviate the false economy of trying to repair and maintain the antiquated structure that we now use as a courthouse."

"From these reports, ladies and gentlemen," the chair summed up in a kindly way, "you can see it is not a question of what we would like to do with this fine old building, it is a question of what we can do—"

"Mr. Chairman," said Cousin Willy, stepping with some chilliness out on to the floor. "Before presenting to you a petition to repair or remodel this building rather than destroy it (a request which would have no validity whatever if that is impossible), I should like to have your permission to read a report on the state of the building by Major Anthony T. Hickock,

United States Army, Corps of Engineers, retired."

"Well," the chair explained with a smile, looking about the courtroom, "of course we don't know anything about this gentleman. But we have no desire to forestall the introduction of any relevant testimony—"

"You've heard of Miraflores Locks, sir, I presume," said Cousin Willy from way up.

The chair gazed off patiently at one of the triple-height windows; "Well, no, sir, I can't say I ever heard of that particular brand."

"Well, have you heard of the Panama Canal?"

"Yes, I've heard—"

"Major Hickock was the engineer in charge of building the great Miraflores Locks in the Panama Canal."

"I see," said the chair.

"He has examined this building from top to bottom, and I should like to introduce his report on the state of it."

"Of course military engineering is a very different thing from civilian engineering; has this man a license to—"

"Mr. Chairman," said Mr. Alsobrook with a well-tempered smile, rising halfway to his feet, "I move that the chair accept the colonel's report in evidence—"

"Certainly," said the chair. "I was just about to say we'd be very glad to add this gentleman's opinion to the two we already have. Will you proceed, sir?"

Cousin Willy unfolded a paper and, nesting his open left hand in the small of his back, he read the report. Major Hickock, in a low-temperature military style, made no attempt to deny the serious shortcomings of the building. "That the structure should have been allowed to deteriorate to such an extent as now to make necessary these extensive repairs," the major permitted himself to observe, "is a matter of apparent negligence concerning which it is not my duty to report—"

Cousin Willy's reading was here interrupted by a rustle of feminine applause, which he acknowledged on behalf of the major with a nod or two. The substance of the rest of the report was that not only was the building "by no means beyond repair," but that to destroy "such a dignified and harmoniously-proportioned structure was something which, in the opinion of the writer, the legitimate pride of a municipality in its monuments should go to great lengths to prevent."

The applause that followed this conclusion was more of a downpour than a rustle.

In a minute the chair rose and tapped a few times on the table with an everything-in-its-stride gavel: "The council will be glad to take this report under its due consideration."

"Mr. Chairman," said a voice from the middle of the audience. It was the young man from the WPA. It seemed to me unfortunate for Cousin Willy that he hadn't coached the young man on the best moment to speak out, but that was too late now.

"Yes, sir," said the chair, pointing the gavel at him like an auctioneer.

"Just a minute, Mr. Chairman," said Cousin Willy. "I believe I have the floor."

"I thought you had finished," said the chair, with perhaps what I believe is called autonomic thinking.

"No, sir, I have not finished." Cousin Willy pushed the young man back into his seat with a baleful stare. "With this report on record showing the repair of the building to be feasible, we may now ask what, under those circumstances, is the desire of the Citizens of Fredericksville. Since it is practical either to destroy the building or repair it, what do the Citizens want done with it?—As an indication of what they want, I should like to present to you, Mr. Chairman, a petition calling for the preservation of the courthouse, signed by five hundred and eleven voters and taxpayers." He marched out and laid the handful of mimeographed sheets on the table before the clerk.

"Thank you," said the chair, perhaps with some hypocrisy.

"The preservation of the courthouse being then, in the first place, practical, and in the second place, desired by the Citizens, I should like to ask, Mr. Chairman, on what grounds do you base this plan for destroying the old landmark?"

"The answer to your question, sir, is very simple. First, the three opinions we have heard on the practicability of repairing the building stand, one in favor of repairing, two opposed. The consensus of the opinions so far expressed is that repairing is not practical."

There was some applause at this from what seemed to be the neighborhood of the young man from the WPA.

"Do you mean to say, sir—"

"Pardon me, I have not finished.—As for the claim that a petition signed by five hundred citizens should be interpreted as the desires of a city of eighty thousand,—why, even if it had been signed by five thousand citizens—" He smiled and wiggled the handle of the gavel round at the middle of the audience like somebody delving about in a wastebasket for a discarded receipt: "Did somebody back there have a question—"

"Mr. Chairman. These people who want this old rubbish pile propped up, they don't have to work here."

It was the young man from the WPA and in my first astonishment I thought he had simply double-crossed Cousin Willy. He went on: "They don't care anything about the working conditions of the laboring man. This old wreck is dangerous. It's a fire trap, the ceilings are falling in, a good gust of wind would knock down two or three chimneys—"

"All that can be repaired," Cousin Willy struck in, but the young man went on with rising emphasis.

"All these people care about is having something pretty to look at as they drive past in their limousines. They don't care—"

"Young man," said Cousin Jennie, who runs a boarding house in a good neighborhood, getting to her feet, "did I hear you say limousine?"

"I said limousine."

"Thank you. I just wanted to hear the word again; it's been so long."

There was considerable disturbance after this as Cousin Jennie got her pocketbooks and glasses and umbrellas triumphantly settled in her lap again. And the spirit of decorum was not improved by old Mrs. Julian piping across at Jennie, "The last limousine I rode in, Jennie, belonged to the undertaker at Uncle Jesse's funeral." She gave a sort of squawk for exclamation point and her new teeth gleamed in the murky light.

The chair, sensing an incipient disaster, banged on the table and the pile of petitions cascaded to the floor. All we needed was to have somebody let loose a cage of pigeons.

When the clerk had gathered up the petitions and things had quieted down again, the young man was seen to be still on his feet: "I insist, Mr. Chairman, that the employees of Habersham County be provided with decent working conditions."

"The gentleman is arguing beside the point," said Cousin Willy; "decent working conditions can be had as well by repairing the courthouse as building a new one. There is no suggestion in any of these recommendations to keep the building as it is."

There was some applause, through which I thought I could distinguish Cousin Jennie's umbrella.

"Mr. Chairman!" cried the young man from the WPA.

But the chair deserted him. "This gentleman has the floor," he said, turning to Cousin Willy as perhaps the lesser of the evils.

I couldn't imagine what Cousin Willy was going to do with it; it seemed to me he had already used it for about all it was worth. But when he spoke it looked for a minute as if he might at last be on his way up Little Round Top.

"Mr. Chairman," said Cousin Willy, "I make a motion that the chair call for a rising vote of those in favor of preserving the courthouse—"

"Second demotion," said Mr. Economy and Mr. Wong in a breath.

"Just a minute, if you please, Mr. Chairman," said the attorney rising to his feet with elaborate good humor.

"Mr. Alsobrook," said the chair, with possibly some of the relief of General Sherman making contact at last with the Federal gunboats off Savannah.

"I consider it out of order to call upon this meeting for a vote on a matter that is entirely the responsibility of the duly-elected county officials. It is their responsibility to provide proper housing facilities for the county government; they may ask for any suggestion they care to, but this committee of citizens is not a legally-constituted body with power to advise the council in the discharge of its duties—"

"Does a gathering of Citizens," said Cousin Willy, "require a government license to vote on a public question?"

The attorney smiled at him amiably: "These gentlemen of the council, Colonel, have been entrusted by the voters with handling the affairs of the county. It is not consonant with the democratic form of government that we all believe in (that we would defend with our very lives, if need be), that they should be swayed by a minority such as this. I do not deny the right of this or any other anomalous body to express its opinion, but that opinion must not be forced upon the council, which has had the benefit of the advice of competent architects and engineers known and respected by all of us; this is not a matter in which a pressure group should try to enforce its will on governmental authority."

"This building," insisted Cousin Willy, getting the far-away look in his eyes, "does not belong to the county council to dispose of as they choose. It belongs to the people of the City of Fredericksville and the

221

County of Habersham,—an army more than five hundred thousand strong."

The attorney broke into the murmur of amazement at this figure; "I am afraid the gentleman's idea of our population is as exaggerated as some of his other ideas."

"The figure," said Cousin Willy, "is highly conservative." I thought I detected a slight dismay among the troops, as if even they weren't sure they could go along with him on this; but he pushed right ahead: "This courthouse belongs not merely to the Citizens of today, but of yesterday,—those Citizens who stood victorious with Captain Rudolph upon the ragged terreplein of old Fort Frederick, who looked out upon the pine-barrens where we are now convened and saw the necessity for erecting upon it a new kind of fort, a fort for the defense of law and order, in short, a courthouse. It belongs to their children and their children's children, who enlarged that building and improved it. It belongs to every Citizen who has trod the streets of Fredericksville before us. It belongs to the Citizens who will tread these streets after you and I are gone, sir.—No, the figure is not exaggerated; the only exaggeration was in naming any figure at all, for the owners of this building are as impossible to number as the generations yet unborn—"

The applause that interrupted him rattled the windows. And the chair, possibly with some well-founded qualms at this fortuitous ringing in of the "little-ones" motif, pulled slightly over on his rudder. "The council is of course interested in the opinions of the citizens; whatever our legal rights, we want your suggestions. It is, however, I feel, inadvisable to call for a vote on the question until all the facts are in evidence.—Whatever is done with the building is going to cost the county (that is the taxpayers) money; it is our duty to take care that this money is well spent—"

"Hear, hear!" said Cousin Willy.

"It is for this reason," the chair went on, "that I want to mention the matter of costs. In order to do the financing of either project we need WPA help. If a grant can be secured from the WPA, it will take care of about a third of the cost. But the WPA is not interested in repairing old buildings. There is every reason to believe that a grant of one third can be secured toward erecting a new courthouse. Nothing at all can be obtained for repairing the present structure."

This sounded to me like the trump card, though it was laid down without much dramatics. It brought quite a noticeable intake of communal breath.

In a minute somebody rose and asked him what was

the approximate cost of the two projects, and he held out his hand to the clerk for some papers: "The approximate cost as figured by the architects is three hundred and seventy thousand dollars for a new courthouse, three hundred and ninety thousand for repairing—"

"You mean it would cost twenty thousand dollars less to build a new courthouse than to repair this one!"

"Twenty thousand on the face of it," said the chair. "When you add to that saving, the one hundred and twenty thousand dollars which the WPA would probably grant, you get a total saving to the taxpayers of something like a hundred and fifty thousand dollars."

It was really pretty much a shell exploding in morale's cockpit. Even Cousin Willy's "Presposterous!" afforded no noticeable relief. To my worn nostrils it had a somehow familiar perfume, and if Dewey had been there I imagine he would have looked over at me and our winks would have collided in mid air.

It was a little as if Singleterry, the star batter on our ball team, after getting two strikes called on him, really collected himself and put the third one into a trajectory that seemed destined for the canal bank. The chair, obviously relieved, set out on a round of the bases more or less for the principle of the thing.

For a minute it looked as if there was a chance the ball might hit the top rail of the fence and bounce back. Cousin Willy said, "What sort of repairs are they that will cost three hundred and ninety thousand dollars? Clearly you can make repairs costing a million dollars, but are they the necessary repairs?"

"They are all contained in this report of the architects, which unfortunately is too long to read. They consist briefly of making the structure fireproof, putting in a new heating plant, new plumbing, rewiring—"

"Was this figure arrived at through competitive bidding on the work?" said Cousin Willy, perhaps faltering a little.

"These are not bids for the work," the chair explained coldly. "They are estimates of the probable cost made by experts in the various lines; bids may run a little less, or they may run a little more.—It is therefore a question, ladies and gentlemen, of whether to repair the building for approximately three hundred and ninety thousand dollars, or build a new courthouse for approximately two hundred and fifty."

One of the Daughters of the War of 1812 rose to say

225

the building should be preserved no matter what the cost, but the morale of the rank and file had undoubtedly suffered.

"I submit," said Cousin Willy, his campaign hat blown away and a shrapnel hole through the side of his shirt, but standing his ground, "that the specifications showing just what these repairs are that would cost this preposterous sum be presented to this meeting for discussion; perhaps some of them can be modified and the cost reduced."

There was a murmur of approval from the troops but it hadn't the spirit it once had. "And I furthermore question whether a new building of the dignity of this one could be built for three hundred and seventy thousand dollars. And no matter how much was spent on a new building you could not buy for it the history that adorns this one; on the steps of this building General Washington addressed the Citizens of Fredericksville. In these rooms the delegates of the young State of Georgia assembled to ratify the Federal Constitution,—and just as the last name was signed, Colonel Armstrong's regiment of Georgia Rangers, drawn up across the square, proclaimed the news to the Citizens of Fredericksville by a salute of thirteen salvos—"

"Unfortunately the county government cannot be

conducted on mere tradition," said the chair with a smile. "We are entrusted with the duty to provide the county with adequate and appropriate means for carrying on its business—"

"Let's have the specifications," somebody said.

Somebody else said, "Has the WPA agreed to grant a hundred and twenty thousand dollars for a new courthouse?"

Somebody else said, "I move that the meeting be adjourned."

"It has been moved," said the chair, "that the meeting be adjourned."

The move was seconded from the vicinity of the jury box and the citizens, somewhat confused by the prospect of having to pay over fifty percent more for an old building than for a new one, made no protest. The councilmen rose as the chair struck the table a final thump, and the battle was over.

. . . . Cousin Willy stood there without moving for a minute or two, like Westmoreland, breathless and faint, leaning upon his sword. I saw Cousin Emma leave her seat and go over and stand beside him, just to be there, not to say anything.

I made my way across to them and stopped on the side of Cousin Emma away from the colonel; I said in a low voice into her ear, "I hope this means he's going to lay off. Steer him on to raising camellias, roses, anything. But let this be a lesson. You can't do anything with these people, they've got too much backing—"

I knew I was talking too much and I shut up. But I was afraid if he kept on he was going to find out who the enemy really was and I didn't—well, I wanted him for his own sake to let good do.

Cousin Emma asked me what I meant by "backing," but I made believe not to hear her and went to the colonel. He didn't seem to recognize me completely, but I spoke to him in my professional capacity and asked him if he had any comment to make for the press. I thought, even at that late date, if he could have answered me with a little Southern humor, all might yet have been well.

But he didn't. The courage (or foolhardiness) to take himself seriously did not desert him for a moment. "You may say," he replied, "that I have nothing but praise for the magnificent behavior of the troops."

CHAPTER X

Bᴜᴛ no matter what arguments and inducements
Cousin Emma might have thought up to offer
him, had she had the chance, they were all, I feel,
automatically neutralized in mass when, pacing the old
breastworks in the early sun of the next day, Cousin
Willy suddenly observed there in the front of his mind,
like a gift from Santa Claus on Christmas morning, a
full-grown idea that had certainly not been there the
night before. He halted at once where he was, under
the cedar tree, and gazed off in a sort of amazement at
the pink road over which General Sherman had not
come.

Even when he had first waked up, it had not been to
look back with any loss of heart on the field from
which his forces had been driven. The capacity to be
discouraged was, he considered, as out of place in a
soldier's equipment as an inner-spring mattress in a
bivouac area; his backward glance at the field had not

been in dismay or even in caution, but in a sober appraisal of error for the benefit of the future.

When Cousin Emma murmured over the coffee that she was glad it was all over, he simply stared at her. "There has been no order to sound retreat," he said; "I am scarcely mobilized."

With which he left her and walked out into the yard. He had no trouble in putting his finger, now that it was too late, on the tactical error that had caused the trouble. It was an error of high command and no one's fault but his: he had withheld his reserves too long. He had believed that mere numbers would carry the day and he had not called up his storm troops, his battle fleet; Clyde Manadue, Sterling—

Then he stopped, for here was this full-grown idea standing there looking at him: Clyde Manadue had said the WPA would grant aid in repairing the library, why had it refused aid in repairing the courthouse?

Why, indeed?—And he went back to the house and drank two cups of black coffee.

Then as a commander might go forth to reconnoiter the site of a coming battle, he ordered his staff car and directed Ninety-eight to drive him to the city. He climbed the squalid stairs of the WPA office of that district and asked a clerk if he might talk to the manager.

Half an hour later he descended the hollowed steps with some satisfaction in the set of his jaw; it was as if his cavalry had returned from reconnaissance with a report not yet confirmed that yellow fever was ravaging the enemy effectives. It was not information to build a plan of assault upon, because it was unverified; but if it could be verified—

"Orderly," said Cousin Willy, "you will drive me to Atlanta."

"To which?" said Ninety-eight.

"To Atlanta!" said Cousin Willy in no tone for trifling.

"We going by home first—"

"We move on Atlanta immediately."

. . . . Two days after the public meeting we carried a nice editorial pointing out that since the WPA had refused to grant aid in repairing the courthouse but would grant aid for a new building, it was unthinkable that even the most sentimental citizen could be visionary and impractical enough to want to spend a hundred and fifty thousand dollars more for a second-hand building than for a new one.

To make doubly sure that the authorities understood his heart was now in the right place, Mr. Hoats asked the council's consent to make a cut from the architect's drawing of the new courthouse. We gave it four columns across the front page, mentioning for good measure that it resembled the old courthouse so closely that you could hardly tell the difference. (There was a slight backfire on this aspect of it because somebody wrote in that if it looked so much like the old one what was the sense of changing, but the letter got blown away.)

In the mean time the Advertising Department was beginning to get a pleasanter expression on its face. For in a sort of test case to see how we might react to a real triumph, the authorities had sent some members of what amounted to its Auxiliary Purchasing Division to Crowmartie's, our principal department store, with the suggestion that there might be a boycott of its Men's Furnishings in the wind. As the Auxiliaries explained, what worried them was that it stood to reason the furnishings could not be of the highest quality in a store that spent as much money advertising its wares to the low-grade subscribers of the *Morning News* as to the better type subscribers of the *Leader*. Obviously, if the wares were all the management claimed, it would pay them to concentrate a greater measure of their appropriation on the higher-class subscribers.

The management readily appreciated the logic of this, and they increased their display in our Sunday issue from three-quarters of a page to a full page. This looked to me as if that two-fifty raise that had been dangling in front of me for so long, retreating and coming nearer but always able to elude me, might be on the way up after all.

There was no need for anyone to advise me not to spend it yet; I had been spending it for years. It is a truth rarely emphasized to the young that a certain percentage of the price asked for any article is to offset the possible success of those people who are going to try to get it for nothing. A customer who pays his bills in full is simply donating to the upkeep of the impecunious. It is, moreover, a well-known fact that the chances of your transferring your trade from one store to another strikes far more forcibly into the manager's breast if you are slightly in his debt than if you aren't, and I have found myself upon many occasions the center of quite a pleasurable celebration upon settling an old account at something like seventy cents on the dollar,—which would have been about the price charged in the first place, had there been no necessity to insure against those customers who carry the principle too far and never pay at all.

At any rate, I had already spent the raise; but it was getting round to being time to propose a cash settlement, and the only chance I saw of that was the raise itself. I mentioned it to Dewey casually, trying to act as if I spoke in fun, though as a jest my heart, naturally, wasn't in it.

Dewey sat there with his head on one side to dodge the cigarette smoke, slitting the morning mail. "I'll take it up with downstairs if you really—"

His voice trailed off and I looked over in some concern to see what was the matter.

He held two or three sheets of stationery in his hand, all neatly clipped together; in a moment he unceremoniously began to read:

"To the Editor,
"Sir:—In regard to the recent assertion by the authorities that the WPA had (1) agreed to grant aid in building a new courthouse, and (2) refused to grant aid in repairing the present structure, I append for your information the following correspondence with the Works Progress Administration, Atlanta.

" 'Colonel W. Seaborn Effingham, U. S. Army, retired,

" 'Fredericksville, Georgia.

" 'My dear Colonel Effingham:—Confirming our recent conversation in this office, the policy of the Works Progress Administration is to accept project applications for the purpose of employing certified labor within cities and counties. We do not, in any instance, specify the type of project which shall be submitted. Applications for remodelling buildings are eligible, as well as projects for the construction of new structures.

" 'No project has been submitted through this office calling for the rahabilitation of the courthouse at Fredericksville, Habersham County, Georgia.

" 'An application has been received calling for the construction of a new courthouse, but this application has been returned to the County Council for further consideration by them.'

"In other words, Sir, the local authorities would seem to be suffering from a considerable misapprehension. The WPA has (1) not agreed to aid in

235

building a new courthouse; it has (2) not refused to aid in repairing the present structure.

"The WPA may therefore be eliminated as a deciding factor in the question of the disposition of the courthouse; for its grants in aid, it is immaterial to the WPA whether the project concerns repair or not.

"And since it was this misinterpretation of the attitude of WPA that caused the Citizens at the recent public meeting to hesitate as to how to cast their vote, I propose that you, Sir, request the government to call a new public meeting—"

Dewey buried his head in his hands. "Give me strength!" he said. I felt like doing and saying the same thing.

"What are we going to do with him?" said Dewey. "Why doesn't the government do something? Have they no means of preserving order and decency in the town? Have we no Assessment Board? Have we no Water Department? Have we no Building Inspector? Is the whole county headed for chaos?"

"When integrity starts running amuck," I tried to observe philosophically, "the resulting reign of terror—"

236

But Dewey was in no mood for generalities: "What's the government going to say when they see these letters?"

I confess my skin changed color at the thought. It was like a loose end of yarn in a sweater; whether Cousin Willy knew what he had hold of or not, if he started really pulling, the whole thing might unravel right off our backs. "There's quite a draft blowing through that window," I pointed out.

"He sent a copy round the corner and they'll print it just out of a congenital orneriness.—Take this stuff round to the courthouse and show it to the council for any comment—"

"Oh, Dewey, for cat's sake!" I said.

"Are you still working on this newspaper?"

"Sure, Dewey, but don't you think we ought to talk to Mr. Hoats first, see what Mr. Hoats says—"

His eyes relented. Wanting to send me off to be mangled was, more than anything else, just the result of the irritation he had been caused, as a dog that has been hurt is likely, without any hatred whatever, to bite even an old friend, and when Dewey gave the thing a second thought he stood up and waved the correspondence at me to accompany him across the hall.

To Mr. Hoats, too, it looked every way but good.

He felt that Cousin Willy was getting to be a public nuisance. "Any responsible citizen ought to have civic pride enough not to go round trying to discredit his elected government. What's the pay-off?"

He looked at Dewey, then at me. Of course I had to shake my head; I couldn't go into my inexplicable feeling that it was all somehow connected with having been laid low on San Juan Hill—

"Is he trying to start a second political party here, with all the waste and extravagance of campaigns and elections, all the inefficiency of spoils and changing personnel? Why, some of these people have been in office since they got out of the fifth grade; they know their jobs. Is he trying to turn them all out on the street in penury—can't they talk to him? Hasn't he got any kin people working for the city who can talk to him?"

I nearly went through the floor; I didn't work for the city but I could see their point of view. I changed the subject: "If you want to show these letters to the council yourself, Mr. Hoats—"

"No," he said modestly, like Caesar putting aside the crown. Then his voice changed into a tone that sounded half revengeful, as if he had caught me trying to lead him into a trap. "Al," he said, "I want you to take this correspondence round to the council for any comment.

We'll plan on running it Sunday,—they ought to be able to think up something in three days."

Dewey, as though he couldn't bear to discommode me, took the letters and brought them to me. "Wear your identification tag," he mumbled at me.

I snatched the envelope from him and went out; I probably should not have snatched it, but it looked now as if I was not only going to miss my two-fifty raise, but might be black-listed by the authorities for bearing such ill tidings and spend the rest of my life under a cloud.

. . . . But as I hastened with dragging heels past the Manhattan Café, thinking of the dear old days of peace and contentment when Cousin Willy was with the Moros in the Philippine Constabulary, I remembered the telephone I had called his house from, that Sunday long ago, and it suddenly occurred to me it might save a great deal of wear and tear if I put my head in the lion's mouth over the telephone.

I went in, hung my hat and coat on an empty chair, and loosened my necktie. Sadie seemed to be on the point of screaming but I gave her a reassuring wave of the hand. I called the courthouse and got Chairman Jeffie on the wire; I told him who I was. "Mr. Hoats asked me to get in touch with you about some correspondence that has just come into the office about the courthouse."

I paused in anticipation of a groan, but he just said, "Well?"

"It seems that a citizen, one Colonel W. Seaborn Effingham," the groan came through pretty distinct here, "has sent the papers a letter he received from the WPA in Atlanta. The WPA contends they have not yet received any application for aid to repair this courthouse—"

"Who said they had?"

I gulped and went on. "They also contend that repair projects are eligible for WPA aid."

"What are you trying to do, put us on the spot?"

"Oh, no, sir," I said. "We've just got these letters and we wanted you to know about them—"

"We're not interested in any alleged correspondence of some private citizen. No copy of it has been forwarded to us; it's just none of our business."

I heard this as I would watch a squirrel slither up a tree,—something completely beyond my own capacities and therefore calling out my honest admiration. Any sound politician, though, must understand loopholes and after a while his eye gets so sensitive to them he can pick one out and be half way through it before the untrained and simple-minded taxpayer even understands he is going to require one; he probably carries a few all-purpose loopholes along with him, as a soldier the incipient fox holes contained in his entrenching tools.

"We have to publish it on account of the paper round the corner," I pointed out. "There may be one or two nosey people who'll want to know where that leaves the government."

"We have no comment to make on any private correspondence of any private citizen—"

"Your position is still that the WPA won't help with repair projects."

"Our position," he said, clearly getting tired of the conversation, "is that a field representative led us to believe the WPA does not want to help repair this courthouse."

"Well, can I quote you to that effect?"

"Certainly not. We decline to comment,—decline to comment at this time."

I thanked him and hung up.

. . . . When I got back to the office the wires were getting ready to close. Having no story to write, I wandered into the teletype room,—wandered in as innocently as a baby will put pins in its mouth.

I wandered in, and I stood there in the pelting chatter, watching the little whirring wheel spell and spell and spell, while my pupils slowly dilated and my shoes fastened themselves flatter and flatter to the floor. I just stood there. Like the councilman, no comment came to my mind that seemed anything like appropriate, and I just stood there looking at the broad belt of copy paper hop-skip-jumping past beneath the wheel: PRESIDENT ROOSEVELT TODAY (the wheel paused perkily for the right word) ASKED CONGRESS FOR AUTHORITY TO CALL THE NATIONAL (another pause, filled with a thoughtful tapping as if it must get this just right,—as indeed it must) GUARD INTO FEDERAL SERVICE—

An old cook my mother used to have, had an expression she brought out when any of us had a birthday. "How the wheel do turn!" she used to say. And "How the wheel do turn!" I said today,—far behind me, in the pauses, hearing, or imagining I did, the flutter of the typewriter keys that spent so much of their life directly above the engaging symmetry of Ella Sue's legs.

2

But I was wrong in supposing the authorities were making no comment; it was not comment as I had known it, but it was comment. In fact, it was comment of about the caliber of a squadron of dive bombers.

We planned to run the correspondence on Sunday, and on Saturday morning in plenty of time for our early edition, the Secretary of the Fredericksville Bar Association had his stenographer call Dewey and tell him to sent a reporter round there.

I went round, practically on the double most of the way. The secretary was partner in the law firm of which the senior was none less than Mr. Alsobrook and the junior a young fellow named Luquire who was beginning at the bottom by going to the State Legislature. A blond stenographer with some of the assurance normally associated with Civil Service employees, interrupted her typing long enough to hand me an envelope.

To be sure I understood, I opened it and read from the long sheet, whose extra inches are in about the same category as the silk hats of old-fashioned politicians:

"At a meeting yesterday of the Fredericksville Bar Association, a resolution was unanimously passed condemning the unwarranted interference of a certain vocal minority among the citizenry with the efforts of the Councilmen of Habersham County to

carry out their duty of providing adequate housing facilities for the county government. The resolution, expressing approval of the plan to erect a new courthouse follows."

The "Whereas's" cracked like a battery of 105mm howitzers: Whereas the citizens of Fredericksville, enjoying the fruits of liberty and democratic government, have duly elected their representatives to the Council of the County of Habersham, Georgia, and Whereas one of the duties of said representatives is to provide adequate housing and shelter for the offices of the government of said county,—and so forth and so forth.

"Sister," I said pleasantly, "names are news and there are no names." She shot me a cold blue look. "We'd like to mention who presented the resolution and who seconded it and who discussed—"

She picked up a phone and said to somebody, "A man from the paper is here and he wants to know who presented the resolution and who seconded it and who—"

There was quite a sustained twittering in the receiver, which she lifted out a few inches from her ear. In a minute she said Yessir and turned to me: "That is the prepared statement for the press and there is nothing to add to it."

"Yes, ma'am," I said, and I left.

A statement from such a leading and learned fraternity as the Fredericksville Bar Association was, as anybody could recognize, news, and we ran it on the lower half of the front page under a two-column head and overhang:

LAWYERS IN SPECIAL MEETING
CALL FOR NEW COURTHOUSE

That was on Saturday. On Sunday morning we had a nice editorial on the civic-mindedness of the Gentlemen of the Bar who did not hesitate to turn aside a moment from their pressing affairs and step forth into the lists to champion the cause of representative government. We went on to point out that here spoke the voice of citizens who knew, the men who used the building, who knew its gross inadequacies. (On the original copy Mr. Hoats had inserted, "who every day risked their lives under its tottering beams," but evidently on reflection he had decided there was no use in falling all over his own feet.)

Over in the "Voice of the People" we led off with a letter from Ty-Ty, Georgia, commending us on our Sports Page. After a second letter calling on the faithful to stop everything and get down on their knees and pray in this hour when the end of the world was in sight, we ran Cousin Willy's correspondence with the WPA, breaking it over to the market page.—You can't help admiring that sort of thing.

The colonel's letters stirred up about as much reaction as a glass of milk. Out of what looked to me like a practically inevitable stall-and-spin, Mr. Hoats had pulled us up and slipped in to a perfect landing,—with perhaps just a slight tear in the port aileron. Even though the *News* gave it a display and Cousin Willy called attention to it in his Sunday piece, it didn't amount to anything.

We had a letter on Tuesday from the League of Women Voters calling on the authorities for some sort of reply and explanation. But by Tuesday there were three other supporting batteries drawn up in echelon behind the Bar Association, all of them firing armor-piercing high-explosive Whereas's and Therefore's at Cousin Willy and his band.

. . . . To Cousin Willy's eye, it must have looked like the ambush of Colonel Iredell on the Beaver Dam Road. From behind every tree and stump and log of the forest which a moment before had seemed alive only with the summer chirping of birds, seethed a mass of painted demons, yelling and screeching in a tongue he didn't understand, charging down into the narrow defile upon his little army of untrained recruits bewildered and dismayed to find that their civilized weapons were practically without effect.

Looking about him, Cousin Willy found things in pretty much of a state. True, a grenadier company from the League of Women Voters was drawn up intrepidly behind him, supported by a crack platoon of the Ladies' Memorial Association; and also standing their ground were a detachment of the United Daughters of the Confederacy and a small force consisting of scattered units of the Daughters of the American Revolution and the Daughters of the War of 1812. But the entire regiment of the men's civic clubs seemed to have been either annihilated or disarmed, together with the Broad Street Association and the Chamber of Commerce; a few individual riflemen of those organizations were firing occasional shots into the melee, but they had lowered themselves so thoroughly behind the rocks and boulders that it was impossible to see even the tops of their heads and whatever fire power they developed was consequently expended harmlessly into the upper branches of the pines. The platoon of clergy, with some dignity ignoring the whole thing, like parents at a children's picnic, had drawn itself up in a slight clearing and seemed to be preparing to pitch camp. The Tax-payers' Association was nowhere to be seen, and even the Good Government Committee was only a shadow of its former self.—It was obvious to Cousin Willy, as it would have been to you or me, that the time had come to throw in his capital ships.

In his quick Estimate of the Situation, what alarmed him a little was the inexplicable fact that the main battle fleet was not already entering the engagement; according to his reckoning, they should have been riding over the horizon before now. He had not been in constant touch with them, but their bearings as of their last communication showed them in line of battle right behind him. Though Clyde Manadue seemed to be having difficulty with his starboard generator, it was not serious enough to cause this delay. For there was not only no faint thunder of their armament yet audible, but he couldn't even make out a smudge from their boilers, which should have been under forced draught and pouring a heartening black cloud into the sky to his rear.

He had Ninety-eight drive him hurriedly to the bank.

"I want to speak to your president, young man," he said. "Tell him it's Will Effingham."

He could see his old friend in there behind the glass partition thumbing through a new edition of Superman Comics. He was considerably relieved that Sterling wasn't doing business on the Ogeechee River; there he was for all to see, and the question of bringing him into the action was merely a matter of straightening out his communications, which had evidently got into a tangle.

He watched the young man approach him, bend over and say something. He started to go in; it seemed foolish to stand on ceremony with somebody he had taught the manual of arms to back in the old Habersham Academy days. But Sterling seemed preoccupied, and he waited.

In a minute the young man came back and leaned over the marble; he said in the low voice in which you mention a shade in the interest rate, "Mr. Tignor will see you back in the directors' room."

"Very well," said Cousin Willy, surprised but not caring, "Where does it lie?" He looked at Sterling beyond the glass, figuring that they might just walk back to the directors' room together. But Sterling was putting on his hat.

"Mr. Tignor looks like he's going out," said Cousin Willy, perplexed.

The young man glanced apprehensively across the lobby of the bank and leaned farther still over the marble; "He'll come in the back way.—If you will just follow me, sir,—good morning, Mr. Buden."

The colonel had hardly been seated at the great oval board long enough to realize he was thinking what a nice table this would make for drawing up some kind of treaty, when Mr. Tignor came in and closed the door quietly behind him. "That office of mine is a goldfish bowl," he said, shaking hands with Cousin Willy and pulling up a chair. "What can I do for you, Will?"

"Well," said Cousin Willy, a little surprised that there should be any question in Sterling's mind as to what he could do, "I need a little help, it looks like."

"Financial, I hope," said Mr. Tignor, in the banker's jest reserved for the highly solvent.

"No," Cousin Willy explained, unconsciously pulling the pin out of a hand grenade, "it's a good deal more important than money."

Mr. Tignor beat a resigned tattoo on the mahogany as if, though he had known Will was going to take him into the stratosphere he hadn't expected to soar into it so quickly. He opened his mouth, possibly with the idea of making a reply though it looked as if he were merely trying to take in more oxygen, then he gave it up and walked down to the other end of the table and took a fly-killer out of a drawer.

"We've talked a good bit, Sterling, at one time and another," Cousin Willy went on, "about the evils of neglect."

"Yes," said Mr. Tignor, feeling a little better, "you've got to have supervision. You can't just buy a stock any more and put it in your box and forget it—"

"That's right," said Cousin Willy. "You neglect something and before you know it, it goes to pieces."

"If you're considering making a will, I'd like to have you talk to our Trust Department—"

"For a hundred years," Cousin Willy continued, holding obliviously to his course, "we neglected our land. And now it is starved out and eroded and—and the Savannah River runs red with its blood."

Mr. Tignor jumped almost as if the burglar alarm had gone off in the vault. Then he recovered himself, as Cousin Willy rose and started pacing the quarter deck. "We have neglected our government, Sterling. You mention that you can't buy a stock and just put it away and forget it, and yet that is just exactly what we've done with our government."

Mr. Tignor reached non-committally across the table and smacked at a fly.

251

"We have neglected what is perhaps the greatest single contribution of the human mind: government. I say 'greatest' because it is the rock that all the other contributions are built on; science, art, mathematics, engineering, they are all founded upon government. Without government, the men of imagination, plotting our course ahead of us through the seas of time, are plotting without a rudder. Just as a nation's wealth, Sterling, comes out of the land, its civilization comes out of its government; if you neglect them, both your wealth and your civilization will drain away.—If a democracy is to succeed, the Citizens must participate in the government. There must be, as you so truly say, supervision—"

Mr. Tignor glanced at his watch. "What do you want me to do, Will?"

"I want you to help us save this fine old courthouse. Not because of the building itself but because the building belongs to the people and the people want it saved. Democracy is a government by the people, not by a clique—"

"Will, let me tell you something," said Mr. Tignor. "Sit down here, let me tell you something.—I've been watching all this to-do about the courthouse. It reminds me of somebody down on the Ogeechee River trying to open a can of sardines with a pocketknife. You going at the thing in the wrong way."

He put his palms together with the fingers stretched out and slapped them reflectively a couple of times: "Back in the 'nineties, in old Pud Toolen's day, I reckon you weren't here then, we were all young and visionary, we got together and formed a 'Committee of Fifty,' and we put old man Wilkes up as a candidate for mayor. And we worked on the thing for a couple of months before the election and we saw we weren't getting anywhere. Everybody knew old man Wilkes couldn't beat Pud Toolen. Pud had a way about him; old scoundrel, if ever there was one, but he was just so doggone nice about it. Do anything for you. Give you the shirt off his back; didn't matter whether he knew you or not. He just loved to do people favors, anybody.—Well, about a week before the election we called a meeting of the Committee. Old man Group was chairman. And when he called the meeting to order he went straight to the point that was on everybody's mind. 'Gentlemen,' he said, 'there's no use in this wide world for us to come here and waste our time trying to figure out some way to beat Pud Toolen. How much is it worth to you in dollars and cents to put Charlie Wilkes in the mayor's chair?'—Well, we figured, and we got together seven thousand dollars. And we appointed old man Group to go round there and talk to Pud. And he went around and he laid his cards right out on the table: 'We can't beat you, Pud,' he said, 'and we know we can't. How much would it cost us for you to get so sick you couldn't make the race?' Pud chuckled; I can see his big old shoulders shaking now. 'How much is it worth to you, Mr. Group?' And old man Group moved over to the table and took the money out of his pocket. He had fourteen new five-hundred dollar bills, never been folded. He dealt them out there in front of Pud one at a time, laying one beside the other, made a sort of fan. When he finished he sat down again and looked at Pud. And Pud said, 'Well, Mr. Group, y'all have bought yourselves something.'—And Charlie Wilkes moved into the mayor's office. He didn't stay there, but he was there for one term."

Cousin Willy shook his head, but Mr. Tignor went on. "If you want to save the courthouse, Will, I imagine you could do it for less than that—"

"No, sir," said Cousin Willy, "that's not the point—"

"I think I'd be willing to make a personal contribution of any reasonable amount anybody else would make."

"No, sir, it won't cost you a cent. All you need to do

is write a letter to the paper as a private Citizen calling for another public meeting in the light of this new information from the WPA. I am going to get half a dozen other letters from people we all know—"

Cousin Willy stopped because Mr. Tignor's mouth had dropped open and his eyes were staring with a sort of glaze at a corner of the ceiling.

"W'y!" he gasped weakly in a minute. "W'y,—don't you know, if I did that, tomorrow morning the whole county and municipal checking account would be closed out—"

"Nonsense, Sterling," said Cousin Willy calmly. "Be practical. What would they do with it? They can't walk round town with the money in their pockets—"

"Do with it! They would take it up the street to Jesse Bibb, that's what they would do with it."

"No, because I'm going to get him to write a letter too."

Mr. Tignor made a courageous effort to laugh but it didn't come to anything.

"They've got to have a bank, Sterling," said Cousin Willy. "They need you more than you need them."

Mr. Tignor stood up and put away the fly-killer. "You reformers, Will," he said with a smile that he meant to be kindly but that turned out to be merely uncomfortable, for he wanted to get out of the directors' room as much as a horse wants to get out of a stall full of hornets, "you reformers have no sense of reality—"

"This is no more a reform," said Cousin Willy, "than replacing a cracked recoil cylinder."

"How's that?"

"It comes more under the heading of repair than reform."

"You don't seem to grasp the hard-headed facts—"

"The hard-headed facts," said Cousin Willy, "are that if you don't repair something that needs repairing you pretty soon won't have it to repair,—and I am surprised, Sterling, you seem too starry-eyed to see—"

"I am very sorry," said Mr. Tignor, turning cool and realizing there is no use arguing with a wild elephant. He rang a bell.

. . . . This jam, however, among the turrets of one of his battleships did not dismay Cousin Willy; there were other powerful units in the battle fleet. He hardly felt, in the stress of the action, the personal wound he had received; he more or less tore a strip off the gray leg of his uniform and bound the scratch, as his grandfather had done at Chickamauga, and continued on his reconnaissance of the forces still available.

When he was piped aboard the other battleship of the Bank-Trust class, his hopes rose again, for the armament was impressive in the extreme. One glance into the great bright barrel of the safe-deposit vault was itself enough to hearten him; obviously, the muzzle-velocity that could be developed there would be simply annihilating. It alone would restore the situation.

But the real cause of his renewed hope was the belief that, since the prime reason for the jam on the Farmers was the fear of losing the Home Folks checking account, this reason could hardly apply to the sister ship which didn't have any Home Folks checking account to lose.

But when he presented his Estimate of the Situation to Mr. Jesse Bibb and Mr. Bibb, smiling a little into space, removed his horn-rimmed nose glasses and rubbed their edge slowly up and down in front of his ear, Cousin Willy had the first of his misgivings. The difficulty, in a word, was that though Mr. Bibb had, in truth, no government checking account to lose, he had some reason to hope that before very long he would have. Steps had already been taken to invite one of the barbers on the Board of Aldermen to be a member of the Directorate and Mr. Bibb believed that in time things might improve.

Mr. Bibb leaned over within a foot of the colonel's ear. "You are making a great mistake, Will, to antagonize these people," he said, glancing about him.

"Antagonize them!" cried the colonel, lifting himself to his feet with a bang of his stick on the floor that started the bank detective sauntering back toward the president's office. "Are you advocating appeasement?"

"You don't seem to grasp, Will," said Mr. Bibb, "that I have a duty to my stockholders. It is up to me to protect their investment, not to jeopardize it. What of all the widows and orphans who own stock in the bank—"

"What of all the widows and orphans who own stock in the City of Fredericksville!"

Mr. Bibb shook his head hopelessly. "There's no stock in a municipality, Will."

"Every child in this town represents an interest in the future of Fredericksville."

"There you are," said Mr. Bibb. "First you talk about stock, then you talk about interest. Stocks don't bear interest.—That's the trouble with you reformers, Will—"

"How is it, Jesse, you think so badly of this town as not to believe it deserves the best?"

"Of course it deserves the best!"

"But you will not fire one small charge to improve the management of it—"

"What you propose," said Mr. Bibb stiffly, "is that I stab our stockholders in the back. That, I most assuredly will not do. Why, do you think our depositors would ever have entrusted me with their money if they thought I was going to try to overthrow the government!"

"What are you afraid of?" Cousin Willy demanded. "No Citizen has anything to fear from a politician. What Citizen cannot face an investigation of his acts with a clearer conscience than the normal politician? How come the Citizens should be blackmailed into impotence by people more guilty than they—"

Mr. Bibb got up in silence and opened the door of his office. The colonel clapped his helmet on his head and marched out.

. . . . And so the news was borne in upon Cousin Willy that another unit of the battle fleet was out of action. He strode across the sidewalk at his full height, not to betray anxiety to his command; but once within his automobile he allowed himself a moment's weakness and sank into a corner of the back seat,—Ninety-eight assuming the position on the curb of one of the sentries in front of Buckingham Palace.

There was no denying the fact that his reserves had, to express it in the spirit of a friendly communiqué, suffered some damage. Truth to tell, if the situation were being interpreted by enemy propaganda, there was enough evidence to claim his reserves had been wiped out. And truth to tell, also, there were some grounds for claiming that the Commanding Officer had himself again been slightly wounded,—perhaps more than slightly—

He didn't know quite where to turn. It was a waste of valuable time to go to Clyde Manadue; he would have braved the coolness that had settled between them if there had been anything to gain, but he was certain there was not. Still, he needed somebody with influence, with fire power, somebody to provide a firm rallying point—

Then, chancing to turn his head, he saw, over beyond the Doric solidity of the bank, the point of a spire. He lifted his chin and opened his eyes; he could feel a sudden new life surging into his veins. It was like glimpsing through the autumn mists hanging over the Valley the leading guidon of a brigade of Jeb Stuart's cavalry. There was influence, there was a rallying point,—a spire, signifying hope, aspiration, pointing away from the earth in acknowledgment of man's eternal faith in the future, of man's eternal spirit.

He followed a Negro servant in bedroom slippers into the somber study of the Reverend Tillman Yearns and accepted a seat in a wooden rocking chair. He explained the situation and Dr. Yearns listened to him, tapping the balls of his extended fingers lightly against each other and pulling them apart as if they were slightly sticky, gazing over them at a colored picture of the head of Christ in a halo of thorns.

When he had finished the clergyman said to him with a patient smile, "My answer to you, sir, is contained in the twenty-second chapter of the Gospel according to Saint Matthew, the fifteenth verse."

Cousin Willy felt like a pupil at the Academy about to be quoted an elementary theorem in geometry that he had stupidly overlooked.

" 'Then went the Pharisees,' " said Dr. Yearns, " 'and took counsel how they might entangle him in his talk—' "

"I'm not trying to entangle you," said Cousin Willy.

But Dr. Yearns continued with a wary smile, " 'And they sent out unto him their disciples with the Herodians, saying, "Master, we know that thou art true, and teachest the way of God in truth, neither carest thou for any man, for thou regardest not the person of men. Tell us, therefore, What thinkest thou? Is it lawful to give tribute unto Caesar, or not?" But Jesus perceived their wickedness and said, "Why tempt ye me, ye hypocrites? Show me the tribute money." And they brought unto him a penny. And he saith unto them, "Whose is this image and superscription?" They say unto him, "Caesar's." Then saith he unto them, "Render therefore unto Caesar the things which are Caesar's, and unto God the things that are God's." When they heard these words they marvelled, and left him and went their way—' "

"I'm not trying to entangle you, sir, but if these people are allowed to destroy the courthouse against the will of the Citizens—"

" 'In my Father's house are many mansions,' " Dr. Yearns reminded him, emphasizing "many." "Nothing is perfect, sir, in this world below. Only in the world to come have we promise of perfection. 'Lay up your treasure in Heaven where rust doth not corrupt, neither do thieves break in and steal—' "

"But isn't there anything you are allowed to do to help improve things down here below?"

"Put your trust in God, believe in prayer. The

prayer of a righteous man availeth much. We are weak, we are only children in the sight of God. We were conceived in sin, there is no health in us.—And aside from all that, sir, the businessmen in my flock would not countenance the church taking part in politics."

"This is not politics," said Cousin Willy. "This is just the life of the community. This is just ordinary civic cleanliness, which must certainly be next to civic Godliness. This is just as elemental as picking up trash that falls on your front doorstep, as putting on a clean shirt, as putting a new coat of paint on the vestry door—"

Dr. Yearns leaned over eloquently: "Mr. Doc Buden is one of my vestrymen—"

. . . . Cousin Willy went out and sat down again in the rear seat of his car. He took off his helmet and passed a great linen handkerchief over his chin and cheeks and far back over the crown of his head; then he sat there with the handkerchief drooping out of his hand.

A king sate on the rocky brow Which looks o'er sea-born Salamis—. He wasn't a king, but he had counted his ships as the king had. He had counted them at break of day— And when the sun set, where were they?

And when the sun set,—but this was no time for

despair. Even the Tory Colonel Brown in Fort Frederick had not despaired: "It is my duty, as it is my inclination, to defend this post to the last extremity." Some might tell him this was the last extremity, but—there was one thing more he could do. He could go see Clyde Manadue.

He hated to do that. Clyde had been very cool to him since the incident at the library. And with that incident as a guide, was there anything possibly to be gained from talking to him? Cousin Willy wondered if he was just trying to justify to himself not having the courage to go and talk to Clyde again. Maybe nothing was to be gained by it, but the only risk was a wound, and when you get to be sixty-five what was a wound more or less? It was his duty, as it was his inclination, to defend this post—

He asked in the outer office if he might see Mr. Manadue. While he was standing there Clyde caught sight of him through the open door and to his surprise called to him heartily to come on back.

"I'm glad to see you, Will," he said. "This is really a coincidence. I was just signing a letter that might interest you. It's to the War Department."

"Is that so?" said Cousin Willy with the least hint of nostalgia in his voice.

"Let me read it to you," said Mr. Manadue, comfortably proud.

Cousin Willy sat down and crossed his hands on the top of his stick.

" 'War Department, United States Government, Washington, D.C., Gentlemen. I am sixty-four years old, white, Anglo Saxon, in good health—' "

He was offering his services to the government!

Cousin Willy listened, not only with a warm pride in this gesture of patriotism on the part of his old friend, futile though Cousin Willy knew it was, but with a brightening spark of hope which he hardly dared allow himself to contemplate for the outcome of the action more immediately at hand.

" 'You gentlemen will know better than I where I can best be of service, but if my wishes have anything to do with your decision, you will assign me to duty on board a battleship, or preferably, with the tanks—' "

Cousin Willy could hardly contain himself. "Clyde, I am deeply impressed," he said honestly.

"I want front line duty," said Mr. Manadue.

Was it possible, then, that here all the time was the help he had been looking for! Here all the time, while he had been wasting his breath on these others, was a man ready to give up everything to serve his country,

265

ready to face the incredible hardships of combat in the tank corps—

"Allow me to congratulate you, Clyde." He held out his hand. "Yours is the same spirit in which McIntosh replied to the overwhelming British forces demanding the surrender of Fort Morris: 'We, sir,' said Colonel McIntosh, 'are fighting the battles of America, and we therefore disdain to remain neutral till its fate is determined.'"

"Thank you, Will," said Mr. Manadue modestly. "I am only offering to do my duty—"

"Yours is the spirit we need in America today, willing to do anything, go anywhere,—go nowhere, even. You would be willing, Clyde, I presume, to go nowhere—"

"How's that?"

Cousin Willy took a deep breath. "Frankly, Clyde, you and I are about the same age. The War Department is through with me and I doubt if they will be able to accept your generous offer. But you have no idea how pleased I am that this is the way you feel; I was getting a little discouraged," Cousin Willy smiled, "though I am ashamed to admit it. Because, though we may be a trifle old for duty in the field, there are pressing dangers crying for our swords at home. I have been looking in vain for a Citizen with your spirit."

"What's on your mind, Will?"

Cousin Willy got to his feet, his weariness gone, and pacing back and forth, explained to Mr. Manadue what he had explained to the others: the necessity for vigilance, the evils of neglect, the importance of municipal governments as the roots of all government, the courthouse as the symbol of the will of the people. "Call in your sentries," said Cousin Willy, "and the enemy appears—"

"Courthouse!" said Mr. Manadue. And the tone stopped Cousin Willy in his tracks.

"All you need to do," Cousin Willy continued resolutely, "is to write a letter to the paper as a private Citizen—"

"W'y!" Mr. Manadue gasped, the words knocked out of him. "W'y!—"

"But that's nothing, Clyde. Compared to the rigors of actual combat you are ready to undergo—"

Mr. Manadue threw up his hands: "You said you were made of dreams and the Lord knows you spoke the truth—"

. . . . I happened to come upon him a few minutes later.

More or less upon the recommendation of President

267

Roosevelt, I had decided to sell some of my belongings and I was walking down Cotton Row from Harry's, where I had just parted with my bicycle. I recognized Ninety-eight from across the street, though I don't know what it was I found familiar about him, for his figure seemed now never to have known anything like snap and buoyancy. He was standing by the open door of the car looking up and down the sidewalk, his chauffeur's cap in his hand.

"The colonel ain't so good," he whispered to me, somehow seeming, himself, at home in the face of trouble, somehow saying to me that he was a colored man and trouble was his element, somehow saying, "We've been good losers in the game of life—"

I got in the back seat and sat down beside Cousin Willy. He didn't pay any attention to me, simply let me sit there as if I had just been away for a few minutes. He looked broken and he was muttering softly to himself, holding the pith helmet in his lap. I was getting pretty worried about him.

Then I began to distinguish some of the words he was using and I felt better. He was cursing, a long even ribbon of curses that I felt represented the accumulations of a lifetime; they were the curses of a man for the bullet in his thigh, for the subordinate who has failed him,—they were the curses of McClellan on the Peninsula for the War Department.

After a while it gradually began to come out what had happened. "And I blame myself too. I have committed the unpardonable error of overestimating our own strength."

I felt sorry for him. The only help I could think of at the moment was our normal Southern first aid. "Drive us round to Dunavant's," I told Ninety-eight, and I ordered us three bottle dopes.

"Perhaps it's not as bad as it looks, Colonel," I said.

He shook his head. "Albert," he said, after a couple of minutes, "there is only one phase of the whole campaign I can look back on with satisfaction."

I was glad he was now able to find that much and I encouraged him to speak of it.

"When I first saw you again, Albert," he said, gazing up the street, "I must say you seemed as indifferent to the fate of Fredericksville as all the rest—"

"Well, sir," I put in.

"But then, as you began to consider more of the life story of Fredericksville, to realize the inestimable toil and blood and sorrow that Fredericksville has grown from, has fed on in its fertile history, your indifference began to leave you." I looked at him, but I didn't know

269

where to start interrupting him. "And now that we have come to a time of new growth, and toil and blood and sorrow are again called for,—I am proud, Albert, that you have stepped forward into the Guards among the first—"

I tried to protest this unjust praise but he only mistook it for a becoming modesty and hurried on.

"And the same is true of your comrades in arms.— I am planning to talk to them for a moment at the entraining point and I want to show them how they have come forward now as their fathers came forward before them; I want to show them—"

"I'm glad you are going to make us a talk," I said, relieved that his thoughts seemed to be turning ahead of him again.

"I haven't been formally invited yet, but I told Captain Rampey I wanted to say a few words.—I want to point out to them how they have volunteered to serve their country in war, and when they return they must volunteer to serve their community in peace. They must come back prepared to confront every enemy of progress, wherever he shows his head—"

"You didn't tell Captain Rampey what you were planning to say—"

"Certainly. He asked me.—And I want to say to

them this: 'Lads, don't let the fear trouble you that in your hard times you may not be strong. Your fathers were strong. You can be strong too—' "

I was glad he seemed to be more—I was about to say more his real self, but Lord knows there was nothing real about it. But he did seem somewhat more normal and in a few minutes I left him.

3

There were quite a few people at the railroad station to see us off, though there was no way of telling how many had come because of us and how many because of the, to us Georgians, well-nigh irresistible perfume of the spiced pigs sizzling in the blue smoke of the barbecue pits at one end of the station. Anyway, as we swung into the square behind the earnest discords of the Shriners' Band, they gave us quite a nice smattering of applause.

We stacked arms on the exhausted grass, unslung equipment, and were ordered to fall out and stand by, —which we were glad enough to do because we were Georgians and it was after dinner time and the weak September breeze was fanning the perfume in our direction.

They were sending us off in style all right: an official 'cue by resolution of the Board of Aldermen, a couple of official kegs of beer by courtesy of the County Council, music, a yellow-pine speakers' stand with crossed flags on the front under the great seal of Georgia. It had all the makings of a political rally and I felt a little strange to have a bayonet and a canteen on my hip instead of my trusty pencil and a batch of copy paper.

Near a corner of the stand I saw the corn-colored straw hat that wasn't really big but that had begun to be such a blind spot to me on that fatal day at the courthouse. "Well," I said, "you've come round to cover the story, have you?"

"You don't think I came round here to see you, do you?"

This had a certain quality about it that warmed my heart. I don't know what it was about Ella Sue and me; we nearly always got off on the wrong foot. If it was to be different this time, I should almost regret it. "Let's get something to eat," I said.

We walked over to the long table where Buddy Wop was serving the barbecue. "Have you any statement to make for the press?" she said.

"Only that I wish you would convey to our civic

272

leaders my heartfelt appreciation of this young spiced pig,—without which, Democracy as we have known it—"

We found a spot in the shade and she sat down while I fetched us a couple of paper cups of beer. When I handed one to her she smiled at me; we always seemed to get along fine until somebody said something.

We sat there for a while enjoying a very interesting silence, then we were interrupted by the music's abruptly running dry. Mr. Alsobrook announced with a comfortable gravity that we should be led in prayer by the Reverend Tillman Yearns.

Dr. Yearns rose, stretched out his pale hands and closed his eyes. "Our Heavenly Father," he said, "on this solemn occasion of sending forth our young men to be trained for the defense of our great country, we pray Thee to bless each and every one of them, to keep them pure in heart and in deed. Keep strong in them and in us the ideals by which we live. Protect our heritage of democracy now threatened upon the far-flung fields of battle and bring us an early peace that will stop the booming of these guns that are the death rattle of our civilization, a peace in which all people throughout the years to come may live in freedom, with liberty to say what we believe—"

"Where's Colonel Effingham?" Ella Sue whispered to me, nodding at the speakers' stand.

He was certainly not there. But I hadn't expected him to be there. "Were you expecting the colonel to make a farewell address to the troops?"

"Well, this is a military occasion; he's an old soldier. Why shouldn't he?"

"Ella Sue," I said, "it's too bad you haven't been with us all summer—"

She gave me an icy look and I was glad to be interrupted by the applause which greeted the mayor.

His Honor read his speech with a good deal of feeling, finally ending up on his keynote: "And if the occasion arises, what man will not fight for his ideals! We, the people of this community, are blessed by living in a democracy, a free country, and even though at times we are not alert in showing our loyalty to country and devotion to freedom, we do appreciate it. We well know that the ideals of freedom and the free spirit of men lie crushed in other lands, and in this great America, in this great State of Georgia, in this great City of Fredericksville (because we are all one in America today), the ideals of freedom are again in jeopardy and the fruits of liberty do not grow in gardens of tyranny. As Christians, we recognize that the paths leading to

274

righteousness and peace throughout the world are, on the one hand, our petitions and prayers to Almighty God, and on the other, the spirit of sacrifice and courage as exemplified in these young men going forth in the determination to protect and preserve our way of life, to protect and preserve the ideals of government by the people, for the people, and—"

"You've got quite a schedule ahead of you," said Ella Sue.

I could feel the eloquent beers under my eyebrows and I said, "God bless and keep us in this, the political machine age of mankind. God preserve for us our sacred right to indifference.—Ella Sue?"

She looked at me.

"You know, I think you ought to hang a star on the door of the Society Office."

"Why?"

"You got me into this."

"Got you—"

"I thought you would like the uniform."

She gazed down for a moment at the foam in the paper cup. "Why, Albert,—this is so sudden."

We laughed about it, of course, dipping our earnestness in humor, Southern style, as we fry our chickens in batter.

Fortunately, some people near by shushed us and we turned to the ringing tones of Mr. Sterling Tignor, who was sending us off to glory, "even perhaps to make the supreme sacrifice," in defense of our ideals, of our way of life, of our homes.

Then a right curious thing happened. The word "homes" evidently suggested to Mr. Tignor a further elaboration, and he said (and it was the last thing he said), "And, boys, I can promise you this: you can count on the folks at home. When the war is won and you come marching back in triumph, the home folks will be right here waiting for you—"

Somebody in front of us laughed, then somebody over to the right. Then somebody applauded, a little too loud. Then somebody whistled through his fingers. Mr. Tignor held out his hand for quiet, but what with the two kegs of official beer and the fact that we had been listening a long time already, and one thing and another, the uproar seemed to begin to feed upon itself, and, added to the whistles and the whines, you could now hear the rumble of people moving about, getting to their feet.

"Maybe more people heard Colonel Effingham than he thought," I said to Ella Sue. But she was watching it all with a young reporter's eye,—blissfully ignoring

276

the obvious fact that it would never see the light of print.

Mr. Tignor looked back at the mayor and Mr. Alsobrook. Mr. Alsobrook was smiling good-naturedly, as if it were all just a part of the program, but the mayor did not seem very happy about it. Then, as things showed no signs of straightening out, he leaned across the Reverend Tillman Yearns to our Captain Rampey, who was seated beyond him.

This ended the little incident, of course; in fact, it ended everything. Captain Rampey blew his whistle, and in a minute, the sergeants began blowing theirs. The boys up-ended their paper cups and began heading for the lines.

"Good-bye, Ella Sue," I said. I felt myself on the point of making some inane remark, but somehow I didn't. There was a blank moment there in which I don't remember anything, then a moment which is as vividly clear to me as the tremendous one on the courthouse roof. But the detail that has remained the brightest with me is, how shockingly unfamiliar Ella Sue's body was in my arms, unfamiliar in exactly the way her legs had been, resolving from the mere body of any girl to Ella Sue's. And I thought what a complete and composite fool I had been all these weeks.

"Why didn't you tell me, Al?" she said.

"I reckon I couldn't figure out how to say it without getting serious."

"Seriousness won't bite you."

"I'm a Southerner, darling," I laughed, "and I'm scared to death of it."

The hoarse sergeant-shouts pulled me away from her and I landed in my niche in the rear rank under a detailed scowl from Sweetie Pie. As we faced right and got under way to march to our train, the Shriners stood up and gave us "Dixie," and the mayor, now fully recovered, came to the front of the stand and, leaning over the great seal of Georgia, clasped his hands above his head in a final gesture of farewell and congratulation and hurry-back.

When the train started moving, I hung out of the window, waving like all the rest, trying to get a last glimpse of Ella Sue; I wanted to tell her, before she decided that seriousness wouldn't bite she ought to talk to Cousin Willy. I couldn't find her and I couldn't have hollered all that at her anyhow.—But while I was still looking, as my car rolled heavily across a street intersection, I saw the colonel.

He was standing on the cobblestones in the street beside his automobile, standing by himself and standing at attention. There were saber-edged creases in his fresh khaki and he wore his ribbons; his cheeks were shaved pink and I am sure his fingernails were trimmed to a thirty-second.

I tried to attract his notice but of course he couldn't distinguish me from the others; he just stood there, gravely and with an indefinable respect, watching us leave. Then as the last car came abreast of him, romantic and sentimental to the end, he brought the straight brown fingers of his right hand to the visor of his cap and held them there while the car passed,—no doubt murmuring to himself, "Don't let the fear trouble you, lads, that in your hard times you may not be strong. Your fathers were strong—"

As well as I could, what with leaning out the window, I gave him my Number One salute,—as a patrolman ran up to him and hustled him a little to one side, clearing a path for the long black automobile bearing His Honor the Mayor and his Distinguished Guests.